Summer Solstice 2012
Sue Peterson's
Book Club

W(A)N T E D :

E L E(V)A T O R   M A N

D0027246

Joseph G. Peterson

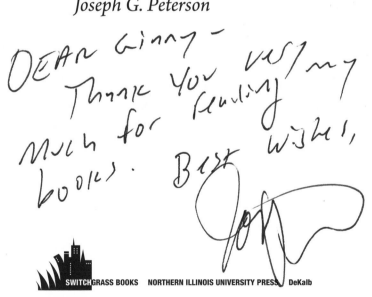

Dear Ginny —
Thank You very much
Much for reading
books. Best Wishes,
Joe

SWITCHGRASS BOOKS   NORTHERN ILLINOIS UNIVERSITY PRESS   DeKalb

© 2012 by Northern Illinois University Press

Published by Switchgrass Books, an imprint of Northern Illinois University Press, DeKalb, Illinois 60115

Manufactured in the United States using acid-free paper

All Rights Reserved

Design by Shaun Allshouse

Library of Congress Cataloging-in-Publication Data

Peterson, Joseph G.

  Wanted: elevator man / Joseph G. Peterson.

pages cm

Summary: "A profound but comedic meditation on failure in this life, how one comes to terms with not achieving one's dreams, the nature and origin of such dreams, and the meaning of the American dream itself" — Provided by publisher.

ISBN 978-0-87580-677-8 (pbk.) — ISBN 978-1-60909-056-2 (e-book) (print)

1. Losers—Fiction. 2. American Dream—Fiction. I. Title.

PS3616.E84288W36 2012

813'.6—dc23

2011044761

WANTED:

ELEVATOR

MAN

For Anna Genevieve and Lily Blanche

WANTED:

ELEVATOR

MAN

Shantih shantih shantih

—T. S. Eliot

1

One morning, age twenty-nine, Barnes woke from troubled dreams and was assailed by a crisis of confidence. It had come over him like a deluge . . . this despair. Retrospectively, Barnes thought it was funny how one morning he was fine but next morning paralyzed with such depression he couldn't muster the strength to get out of bed. No matter that he had a nice job waiting tables. No matter that North Dakotan loan companies from his student days had come after him for being chronically delinquent with his payments. His body and mind had said, in the vein of Bartleby, I prefer not to.

For months after that fateful morning, his mind felt like soup, his soul even soupier. He cried soupy tears, and when his tear ducts ran barren he endured months of dry heaves—crying and suffering for what he couldn't say. Sure, he'd never known his father—wasn't even certain whether he was alive or dead. There had been an urn with ashes, tucked away in his childhood home, and he supposed, at some level, that maybe those ashes had once been his dad, though his mother had always claimed the opposite—

that they were the ashes of Smoke, a loyal mongrel bitch that had followed her through her childhood, which had been a lonely, bitter childhood lived on an isolated farm in the middle of the Iowa Steppe.

His mom had never completely lost her bitterness. She was proud to a fault and had always seemed too cold and too calculating for the small Iowa town in which they lived. She never mentioned his dad, and Barnes had, only once or twice, attempted to broach the subject. But his efforts produced no results. One day, however, when he was twelve, apropos of nothing, she broke her long silence on the subject and merely said, "My child, I will tell you this once and once only. Your father and I were never very close. He was a generation older than me—and when I met him, he was a professor at Iowa State. I was a student of his. He was a highly brilliant scientist, not particularly handsome, who flattered me with his intentions. I allowed myself to be flattered. But he never understood me. I didn't understand him either, so fair is fair. He had charisma. People liked him. He had enormous ambition as well. He was highly successful. He was one of the scientists who worked on the bomb in Los Alamos, and just after it was dropped he went to Hiroshima to assess the toll radiation took on the survivors. When he returned he became a pacifist and fought hard to reduce nuclear arms buildup. Just after I became pregnant with you, he met up with someone else, a woman by the name of Nel, and with her he moved to Las Vegas to make his fortune. Whether he's dead or alive, I don't know. The ashes in the urn belong to my old dog, Smoke—and I've kept her with me because I didn't have the heart to bury her."

Another time, two years later or so, she merely said, "He's dead. Radiation poisoning. Your father was a scientist. He flew after the *Enola Gay* to see the effects of radiation on the survivors. He returned and within a few years he was dead. We were never close. He was older. It was a marriage of convenience. We had you, you know. And so, that's about all I can say. Frankly there's nothing really *to* say. What's more, I don't like speaking of all this nonsense. Don't you have something better to do with your time than pester your dear old mom with silly questions?"

When Barnes's mom died, there was the question of the ashes in the urn. Barnes, who was never convinced the ashes belonged to Smoke, didn't have the courage to bury them either. But why was that? What would it have taken to bury what may have been his old man's ashes? An afternoon floating in a boat over some pretty body of water? A brief eulogy? A scattering of dust to the winds? What could have been simpler? Yet he hadn't had the courage and when his mom died just six months ago he merely directed that the ashes in the urn be strewn in her casket and the two of them sent to earth together. Occasionally Barnes was troubled by the thought: What if the urn didn't in fact contain his dad's ashes? What if, indeed, it contained his mother's old pet dog, Smoke, or something else? Wouldn't that mean he defiled her grave? But then he realized that she had kept the ashes for a reason and—whether they belonged to his dad or her dog—he supposed in the end she could do with a little company in the long slow molder to dust.

2

The depression which had overcome him subsequent to her death was something else entirely. It was like an illness, something you catch, and it grabbed hold of him bodily and shook him with visceral force. He felt it bearing down on him from above and drawing him down from below as if he were in one of those centrifugal spinning rides at an amusement park, being addled by a carnival operator who refused to stop the ride.

In the mornings when it was time to go to work like the rest of the world, Barnes merely stayed home, cowering from the world. He lay daily on his old mauve couch, in fetal position, and clicked with growing discontentment through TV channels. Dishes piled high. He'd taken his phone off the hook and lay, week in week out, wasting away in a funk of depression.

Besides a few visits from his ex-girlfriend Mia, a lovely, graceful woman who, Barnes suspected, still loved him, and irregular visits from his upstairs neighbor Tom, a former locomotive mechanic and a mostly solitary drunk, Barnes was remarkably cut off from the world. If I die, he thought, nobody will know the least difference. He kept a pile of razor blades near his bathtub lest something drastic be required. What drastic was, he couldn't quite say—but in dark hours he imagined the worst.

It was during this period of neglect when his ancient Abyssinian cat, Clem, attempted to supplement his diminishing diet with a wayward sparrow. The cat leaped off the back porch and landed, slightly off cue, on his jaw—breaking it. Barnes took Clem to the vet, was told nothing could be done—certainly not for an eighteen-year-old cat—and Barnes was ordered to put him on a special diet, which, Barnes later discovered, broke his budget. After that little incident Barnes called Clem "Crazy Cat"—and instead of the special meals, he spoon-fed Clem baby food from a jar.

Barnes had failed to land on his feet as well. Just when he thought his troubles exceeded his capacity to deal with them, he received a termination notice in the mail. He was canned from the restaurant. His boss, who was an evil, unhappy cur, had written a five-word sentence that smote Barnes as if it had been some potent and irreversible hex: "You're fired, don't come back." It was the cruelest thing anybody had ever said—much less written—to Barnes, though it wasn't the first time it had been said (or written). In the past eighteen months he had been fired from—get this—seven restaurants.

Seven, which had always been Barnes's lucky number, was now a talisman of cosmic failure, which bedeviled him. He called it "cosmic" because if it weren't cosmic then it would have to be karmic—but it couldn't be karmic because nothing he had done either in this life or any previous life merited this sort of punishment. Seven jobs in the last eighteen months. How am I ever going to regain my foothold in the workplace after this cruelest of blows? It was a reasonable question for which Barnes had no reasonable answer.

During this period, Barnes spent long hours scrutinizing his face in the mirror—he had nothing else to do, so why not? He posed absurd questions to himself such as: Am I even fit to be a member of the human race? He invariably left these sorts of questions unanswered. But if you looked closely enough, his face told the tale of his woe. It was a very average face: dark hair, high forehead, slightly curly bangs—which in his childhood had been a cowlick—flat, plain cheekbones, and an arguably Roman nose. His chin protruded mildly, its forward dimension enhanced by a deep cleft in the center. As a child his malocclusion went unchecked by braces; thus he had crooked teeth, which some thought gave him character and others thought marred his thick-lipped smile. Barnes hated the plainness of his face—and once he had even wished he had been born black with a huge untutored Afro and fearsome eyes. But he was what he was, or as he would sometimes say to himself in mock Popeyese: "I yam what I yam." And though he pounded his chest as he said it, he wasn't proud of the fact. His eyes were ringed and sad like a raccoon's, and he was claustrophobic inside his own body.

At night—restless, sleepless, concerned that he was closer to the abyss than he thought—he'd take long peripatetic walks through the neighborhood whistling dissonant tunes, wondering how he was ever going to make it to the ripe old age of thirty. His mind worked circularly at this time of night, the same words churning round and round in his head like stones. He only wondered what precious thing was being ground down to dust by the wearying circularity of his thoughts—his self-esteem, perhaps, or worse, his soul. He threw the words out for all the world to hear: depressed, worthless, underutilized, useless, hapless, waste, garbage, debris, loss.

These words, as well as a handful of others too nasty to print, were words he felt most aptly described him. He mumbled them and sometimes in a fit of exorcism he'd howl them at the top of his lungs. He didn't care what the folks inside all those pretty houses thought of him, if they thought of him at all. He was doomed and damned and most of all neglected. And if they did care to think of him, they realized, before long, that he was nothing more than a harmless madman mumbling monikers in their midst.

Barnes was a man in the prime of his life, and yet for reasons he couldn't entirely explain he couldn't hold on to a job. Harder still was finding a job he actually wanted to hold on to. He had a degree, after all, from a major institution and it seemed that something better than waiting tables should lie in the offing. But so far nothing had come. He applied for a variety of jobs, searched the want ads, hired a headhunter. Nobody out there in the air-conditioned offices of the city wanted his head, so in the meantime he waited tables. And now, when he circulated from restaurant to restaurant looking for a job, he felt like a person in a doomed relationship trying to make something work that was never meant to be, that he himself had never wanted to be.

And then of course there were the interviews with nervous overworked restaurant managers, who seemed able to smell this on him—who wanted to know why he'd been fired from his previous jobs waiting tables. If he didn't tell them that he'd been fired then they wanted to know what he'd been doing with his time the past eighteen months. What could he tell them? That he'd been sitting around his studio apartment obsessively culling the want ads for some opportunity out there that would rise to the occasion of his capacity? And just what was Barnes's capacity? What capacity did you possess if you couldn't even manage to hold on to a shitty job waiting tables?

And so when these nervous managers asked, "What have you been doing these past eighteen months if not working?" he didn't know what to tell them. He merely gave them a blank look and smiled as broadly as possible. He said that he would dedicate himself, if necessary, to doing the best he could servicing the customer with a smile. This response, of course, earned him spontaneous uncontrolled laughter. "And in what way do you propose servicing them? This is a restaurant we have here, buddy, not a service parlor."

3

It was morning when Barnes returned home, exhausted from his walk. The self-help pamphlets were there on his floor mat, and a note was posted on his door. It was a cutout from the want ads taped there by his neighbor, Tom, who only wanted to help. Barnes peeled the ad from his door, stepped inside, picked up a handful of the pamphlets, slumped onto his couch, and began looking over the offerings carefully. The ad read:

Wanted: Elevator Man.

One quality soul needed to fill demanding job on the Elevator Commission. It's thankless, but you will be paid appropriately for your labors. 154 S. LaSalle.

It was an absurd ad, help that didn't help, and Barnes was immediately angry with Tom for posting it on his door. Didn't Tom realize that Barnes wanted something more out of life than a dead-end shift on an Elevator Commission? It was bad enough he had so far only amounted to a "failed waiter," but what on earth was a job on the Elevator Commission? Was it a parallel move? A demotion? A downward plunge into the true abyss? Hell, he'd rather stay unemployed. After all, he had an education from a major institution, which is more than he could say for Tom. But there was something else that occurred to Barnes. Tom needed a job as well. He couldn't collect disability forever, could he? And what was his disability? Alcoholism? Tom seemed more suited for this sort of work than Barnes. So why was Tom overlooking this opportunity and passing it along? Was even Tom too good for such work? If so, wasn't Barnes, by the transitive relationship, also too good for such work? Hell, with Barnes's credentials, surely, he could and should get a job that required him to wear a suit every day. Unfortunately, such work seemed difficult to obtain. Barnes put the ad aside and looked over the self-help pamphlets. Attached was a note written in crude handwriting. "Try these. They must help. Tom."

The pamphlets—most of them decades old, dog-eared, and pilfered from garage and yard sales—came in an assortment of shapes and colors. They were modesty printed on cheap paper, which was brittle and yellowed with decay. His fingers smudged the ink. Nevertheless, Barnes was intrigued by their titles, seeing as they all ended with exclamation points.

How to Jump-Start Your Life!

Ten Easy Steps to Accomplishing All Your Goals!

Gumption: How to Get It After You've Lost It!

Become CEO: 100 EZ Steps!

Opening one of the pamphlets, randomly, he found this tidbit:

Rule Seven: **Admit you're a loser.** What is a loser you ask? A loser is someone who, somehow or another, allows himself to fail, not because he is not capable of success but because he believes that he is incapable of success. It is, therefore, a belief in one's inadequacy that makes one a loser. Admit that you are inadequate, and therefore a loser, and you will begin to regain control of your life.

It seemed a sensible enough rule—one, like so many other rules, that didn't need stating. Barnes chuckled at the advice and wondered at whom—what lost lonely soul—it was aimed and then a moment later, he realized it was aimed at him—at me, he thought. He opened another pamphlet and found this piece of advice:

It begins and ends in the gut. Trust and believe in your gut instinct. If your gut instinct tells you something's fishy in Denmark, then steer clear of sushi while there.

And yet another piece of advice farther down the page:

Believe in Chance! If this pamphlet has fallen into your hands, take it as a good omen and read on! Your future depends on it!

My future, nonetheless, Barnes thought. As Barnes read on he grew modestly impressed, though not sold on the pamphlet's contents. The question always became for Barnes, especially in theoretical matters: Well, but how does it pertain to reality? The rule may be logical—but does it pertain to reality? He had realized, for instance, that in theory admitting "you're a loser" might help, but in reality, it probably wouldn't (for wouldn't it be just like a loser to admit he was one?). And it was this "probably wouldn't" that made most advice seem irrelevant to Barnes. "Believe in Chance!" But reality didn't give a damn one way or another about Chance. Nor, for that matter, did it make exceptions for those who believed in it.

Nevertheless Barnes began carefully reading the pamphlets. He had nothing else to do so why not? He took notes in the side margins, and if he found a rule he thought useful, he attempted to memorize it. Despite the rather thin content of the pamphlets, the endeavor seemed modestly intellectual, and it made him feel better and better every day. Reading these pamphlets became, for Barnes, an exercise akin to work. He'd brave the cold waters of their optimistic know-how can-do advice in the morning. Fighting cross-current against bitter self-loathing, he would apply a sort of scholar's focus in an attempt to decode the self-help language. He'd searched the empty spaces of platitudinous text for hidden meanings and yearned most of all for the holy grail of just exactly how to do it—get gumption, that is, after you'd lost it. In this way, Barnes became a sort of connoisseur of the genre. The pamphlets he liked best came from a firm no longer in business, whose imprint was Success, and the series It's Just Within Your Reach had a bunch of fascinating titles including this one: *Downward, Downward You Go, Which Way Is Up Nobody Knows*. It contained this counterintuitive bit of advice, which Barnes was unable to forget: "Redefine your idea of success! Think downward!"

The question became for Barnes, how should he apply this newfound knowledge? Should he aim high—go for broke—for an office job of some sort? Or should he make a more modest start, say for example, factory work, or a trade—bricklayer, plasterer, electrician—or should he stay in the service industry? But no, the service industry, in light of his most recent calamities, was out of the question.

What to do for a living revolved partly around an assessment of just exactly what his caliber was and partly on what he estimated his luck to be. That's at least what the *Get Gumption* pamphlet argued—and it somehow seemed the most persuasive of all the pamphlets. Some days Barnes woke with rocket fuel in his veins and proclaimed: "The sky's the limit, and my luck, hell, it's bound to upturn." Other days Barnes was so ravaged with the age-old troubles of self-doubt and self-loathing that he didn't have the wherewithal to step foot outside his apartment door. It was all made more complicated by the sense that though he lacked the energy, yet he thought he should do more with his life. He thought of his father—whom he had never known—charting a heroic line following in the jet stream of the *Enola Gay*. His dad had been a man of enormous accomplishment. Perhaps he had died of radiation poisoning. His mother, who had been wounded by his father somehow or other, had always been loath to speak on the subject. And other relatives—well as far as he knew, there weren't any. His father's heroism and pacifism were in turn contradicted by the story that Barnes's dad was a scoundrel, that he had abandoned his family for a more prodigious babe and fortune somewhere in the great neon miasma of the Las Vegasian desert. Either way Barnes looked at it, his father had gone for broke: either as a hero dead at a youngish age or as a sucker caught, planktonlike, in the baleen teeth of Harrah's, pulling a slot handle to save his soul. And if his father had gone for broke—well by god—shouldn't he, too, go kamikaze and brave broke? All or nothing? Top or zero? Throw all the chips down and shoot the craps? And some days Barnes thought, Indeed I should. And most days Barnes, paralyzed by a sense of doom, thought, Indeed I shouldn't.

It was there, in the welter of contradicting emotions about his uncertain past, where Barnes began to fashion a can-do career strategy that seemed to make sense.

"Forget the past," Tom told him, sipping a beer.

Barnes eyed Tom—who had a slight tremor from years of solitary drinking and who occasionally broke down sobbing for no reason—and said, rather caustically, "What do you know about forgetting the past? You've been suffering from nightmares for years."

"Forget it," Tom told him, then added: "Do as I say, not as I do."

"That's exactly opposite the advice Mia gives me."

"Listen to Mia then."

"She says I should remember the past. That's where my strength lies."

"Bully for Mia." Tom raised his glass. "She's a beautiful

woman. I don't know why you don't marry her."

"I don't know why, either," Barnes said. And in truth he didn't.

Tom was right—not about Mia, but about forgetting the past—and Mia was wrong. The pamphlets emphasized this point as well: Forget the past. Admit you're a loser. Move ahead to the thing nearest at hand and build from there. But whatever you do, move forward—*avanti* —into the future. And the future for Barnes meant one thing: getting a job. It had occurred to him suddenly, in a brainstorm he'd had while sulking in front of the mirror, that if he only got inside the entrance of one of those big buildings downtown, then somehow or another sooner or later good fortune might strike. It seemed an asinine strategy at first glance, but the idea's rightness lay in the fact that Barnes had conceived it, all by himself, in the smithy of his soul. Once conceived, he clung to the strategy as a drowning victim clings to a bubble, which is to say he clung to it with vain hope. After all, it was a strategy forged not in some how-to pamphlet . . . but in the heart. And Barnes had always believed that if one does what the heart bids, why then, what could go wrong? And for three whole days he paced the floorboards of his apartment mulling it over, wondering what could possibly go wrong. What could possibly go wrong? What, I ask you, could possibly go wrong? And the answer invariably arrived like thunder: The world could go wrong with you smash-bang caught in the middle. But on the fourth day, a ray of light passing through the torn blue bedsheet he'd hung as a curtain crossed over his face and woke him from deep slumbers. Barnes rubbed his eyes, stretched, and felt renewed. He felt filled with hope and optimism; a raw sexual energy akin to life stirred his loins. What the hell, I'm tired of this funk. It's time it was over. That said, he got dressed, making ready to shove off into the world.

4

His luck changed in a moment. It was a turnaround and it had happened—like all fortuitous events—when he least expected it. He saw an advertisement for a company in need of an elevator man—it was a coincidence because it was the same job Tom had posted on his door several weeks earlier. This coincidence seemed too uncanny to ignore. Or, as he thought to himself in his newly acquired self-help lingo, Ignore this offering at your own peril!

He mentioned all this to Mia, what he called his two-point plan for recovery:

- First I'll get a job in a sky-rise downtown doing menial work like the elevator job,

- then I'll reach out to one of the higher-ups whom I'll inevitably meet in one of the elevators going up.

She listened quietly. He imagined her frowning a tad on the other end of the line, and then tersely she pointed out that it was an okay strategy, so long as he didn't get caught settling for just the elevator job.

"Of course not," Barnes insisted. "Why would I do that? Certainly I merit a job better than the Elevator Commission. I agree with you there. This is only a way into the building. Because look at it this way, Mia. What other way do I have of getting access to the people who go up and down those elevators? In some of those cars are the power brokers. I'll give 'em an elevator speech and before you know it I'll be off the Elevator Commission and on to better things."

"Good. That's the way I like to hear you talk. Do you have your elevator speech planned?"

"Well, to show you I've been thinking about this, I do have an elevator speech. It goes something like this: 'Sir, my name is Eliot Barnes. Currently I work for the Elevator Commission. However, I do have a diploma from a major institution, and as such I believe I can do anything under the sun. Certainly I can wait tables, but I want more than that. In short, I'm eminently trainable. I possess an analytic mind. For goodness gracious, I studied dialectical reasoning with a world-renowned expert in the field, F. R. Thompson. Sir, with all due respect, if you can master dialectical reasoning, I'm sure you'll agree with me everything else in the world is simple as pie.'"

Mia laughed. "You're so silly. But I'm glad to hear you're trying."

5

Hoping the job was still available, Barnes took the bus to the Loop and was pleased to discover that the building that needed his assistance happened to be one of those great gray monoliths lining the canyon of LaSalle Street. He pushed through the revolving door of the building. The interior of the building was as magnificent as a church with a black-and-white marble tiled floor stretching in every direction and marble arches that rose three stories and were capped by austere domes gleaming in hammered gold leaf. On a distant wall was a massive clock, whose sweeping fifteen-foot second hand left the irrevocable passage of time in its wake but not before neatly parsing it in Roman numerals.

Three men in brilliantly crisp suits and perfectly coiffed hair (hedge fund managers by day, triathletes by night?) appeared around the corner and vigorously strode across the floor in his direction. The leader of the three—no older than Barnes with a large mole beneath his eye and dark curly locks—approached, and for a moment Barnes, in febrile state, thought he was going to be offered a job *tout de suite,* on the spot. I knew I should have come here sooner, Barnes thought. This was the perfect strategy. If you want to work in an office building, then you have to actually go and hang out in an office building. Why had no one ever told him that merely reading the want ads or working the phones with a headhunter wasn't enough? Why had no one told him to just pack a briefcase and come on down where the sharks swim? Good thing it wasn't too late. Barnes reached his hand out, ready to shake the hand of the oncoming leader of the group, when the leader's hand reached into his front pocket, pulled out a scarlet handkerchief, and dabbed his brow. The other two men, equally consumed with their important jobs, followed swiftly behind the leader as they breezed past Barnes and out through the revolving door into the canyon of LaSalle Street to accomplish bigger and better things. Barnes stood holding his hand out, then quickly put it back in his pocket. The incident left Barnes, for a moment, stunned. What had he been thinking? Am I an idiot? Did I really think I could come on down here and that someone, some higher-up was going to recognize my implicit talent and hire me on the spot? No wonder I'm hopelessly unemployed. I don't have the wits to go and get a decent job. My instincts are off-kilter. I'm an idiot. And those suits—how did they figure it out so young?

Higher-ups of both sexes strode past on either side of Barnes, oblivious to him. It was spectacular how puny he felt all of a sudden, and insignificant in the great domed cavern of the building. I'll never succeed in this world. They all seemed locked in, networked; they knew where they were going and what they were doing. Barnes felt lost by comparison. He was dazed by the magnitude of his idiocy; then he looked around and remembered why he had come. He fished the ad out of his pocket, consulted with the doorman, who looked ordinary enough even though he wore a red monkey suit with a gold collar tight around the neck. Barnes was pointed to a stairwell in the corner of the lobby that led downward, into the dark bowels of the building.

It was a Gothic, mazy basement that suffered from decades of neglect. It was supported by internal flying buttresses, old steel beams, and pipes with peeling asbestos insulation. In the center of the basement was a small oily shop, closet sized, and through the glass-paned door one could see it was lit with two exposed seventy-five-watt bulbs that dangled from wires at either end of the ceiling. He rapped on the door, waited an uncomfortable moment, was greeted by a tall man with thin limbs and a pale complexion who, like an apparition, appeared suddenly from seemingly nowhere.

"Yes, may I be of assistance?" he asked.

Barnes, a bit daunted by the man's demeanor, unfolded the job notice and in a barely audible whisper said, "This. I've come for this." His caution surprised, if not the tall man standing before him, then himself. Who am I to pay obsequy to this man? He's nothing but a common laborer. But the man's presence had a latent virile reality that was hard for Barnes to ignore.

"This, what's this?" the man asked, snatching the ad from Barnes's fingers. He held it up to the bulb, mused over it long enough to suggest he didn't know how to read, then turned an eye to Barnes. "Step inside." He brushed a seat, indicated that Barnes sit. "You're lucky this position is still available. . . ." The man's voice was high-pitched, nasal, and reedy. "I posted this advertisement weeks ago . . . got dozens of calls . . . phone ringing off the hook . . . all sorts of desperate people, desperadoes, folks with hunger in their eyes . . . others with hunger in their bellies . . . two or three ex-cons stopped by, inquiring . . . one claiming to have been a political prisoner . . . the other claiming to have been innocent of murder. . . . Do I look like an idiot? Do I look like someone who's so easily fooled? I posted the advertisement. I said, '*quality* person needed for *demanding* job . . .' and not one person of quality . . . not one person with aspiration came seeking the job. . . . No one who could fulfill the job's demands answered the call." The tall wan man looked Barnes over carefully. "Are you still interested?"

Barnes, trying to show his finer side, nodded yes and then answered as affirmatively as possible, "If a job is still available, I would like to have a shot at it."

The tall wan man laughed at Barnes's locution. "You'd like to give it a shot, would you? It's a demanding job . . . one that's necessary. We are looked down upon but we . . . there is a brotherhood here . . . we are the ones who make things work . . . we work in the shadows of the limelight . . . but we are not the silent majority . . . nor the wronged minority . . . we are the few . . . the proud. Do you understand what I'm saying?"

Barnes nodded his head yes.

"Good."

He handed Barnes a simple questionnaire, which Barnes, using a blue ballpoint pen that left dabs of ink in its wake, filled out as follows: Did he suffer from claustrophobia? (no). Was he susceptible to motion sickness? (no). Had he ever done janitorial work? (yes). Of course all his responses had been lies. But if lying on a simple application is what it took to get hired, well then, Barnes was prepared to tell a little lie. Miraculously the tall wan man—whose name happened to be Charles Augustus Coneybeare—could tell, just by looking at Barnes, that he had never done a stitch of physical labor in his life. Nevertheless, he had decided, against his better judgment, to take pity on Barnes and he hired him on the spot. Barnes smiled at Charles Augustus. He felt he had met a kindred spirit and he said as nicely as possible, "Thank you. Thank you." He almost added, You've given me a second chance. New hope.

"Be here early Monday morning. We start at seven sharp. Tardiness is not tolerated."

"Thank you," Barnes said. "I'll do my best."

"We'll see about that when the time comes."

Barnes thanked Charles Augustus again, held his hand, perhaps longer than he should have, and headed for the stairwell. He emerged moments later into the lobby. His eyes adjusted to the light. The lobby was empty except for the doorman and a few folks walking off in the distance. He remembered how embarrassed he had felt here moments ago. But now he had a job—so indeed he had played his cards correctly. This was the right way to go after all, he thought. It didn't matter all of a sudden that the job he was offered wasn't an office job, it was a job, and in this day and age a job in the hand was better than two in the bush. Ah yes, another maxim from one of his self-help manuals. When he realized that he really did receive guidance from those dusty booklets—and what was the essence of that guidance if not a questing optimistic spirit—he clicked his heels three times and ran half the way home, filled with something inexpressible, though it was probably an emotion akin to joy.

In the day's mail was a note from his alma mater requesting biographical information. Barnes filled out the form, and when it came to the line about current employment, he wrote, tentatively: Elevator Man.

6

That night he had a small dinner party to celebrate his good fortune. He invited Tom down. He purchased a case of beer, grilled salmon. He toasted Tom's health, and Tom his. Mia called and came over as well, bringing a bottle of champagne. They got drunk sitting around the table. Mia went into his bedroom and passed out cuddling with Clem, Barnes's orange-haired Abyssinian cat. Tom and Barnes stayed up until early morning talking.

"What you need now," Tom said, cracking open a bottle and rubbing the neck, "is to get married."

"Leave me alone about that."

"She's just dying for you to ask her to get married. Isn't it obvious to you?"

"Shut up about that. She's moved on to other lovers."

"Then why is she here?"

"I don't know. I'll have to ask her that one myself."

"She wants you."

"Shush."

"I'm serious."

"So am I."

"You've got a job now. What's to prevent you from settling down?"

"Keep your nose out."

"Suit yourself. Only trying to help."

"Help nothing. You're bothering me is what you're doing."

"Bothering you! I suppose you think my posting that ad for an elevator man on your door was also bothering you. Now look what's happened. You've got the job! Congratulations, my boy. May you do good work."

They tilted bottles and said, "Cheers," then drank into the wee hours of the morning.

When he slipped in under the sheets next to Mia, he roused her awake.

"Have you really moved on to other men?"

"I can't wait on you forever."

"But why are you waiting on me?"

"A thought that something may come of you yet."

"This is exciting, isn't it? A job."

"It's good it's not in another stinky restaurant. Just don't get stuck. Oh, and improve your elevator speech."

7

Even though the elevator job was merely a stepping-stone, Barnes tried to take it seriously. He was, after all, an educated man, having received a BA from a major institution. And, as he so well knew, educated folks went one route—office work—while the rest of the uneducated masses invariably took the scraps, and the scraps, as he understood it, were defined as anything having to do with menial labor. Trying to prove he had ambition beyond such trifling labors, he planned to show up his first day at the Elevator Commission in a suit whose color was described in the sale brochure as being "Universal Blue." Barnes liked the name of the color, not to mention the look, and had snatched it up at a bargain. He wore a white shirt and black tie. He carried an empty leather briefcase with brass latches that clicked open when you pressed a button. On his feet he wore freshly polished wing tip shoes. He had hopes for a grand beginning. If this was a start, he wanted it to be a big start. If it was a first step, he wanted it to be followed by a journey of a thousand more steps (up the corporate ladder, of course). The depression that had knocked him for a loop was gone. And at least until it returned—for didn't these sorts of mortal depressions always return?—he was ready to take the world as it came: head-on.

Mia was up early and cooked him breakfast.

"It's early, Mia; go back to bed. You don't have to cook me breakfast."

"I want to see you off. And see how you look in your new suit."

His suit smelled clean. With its sharp crisp edges and slightly padded shoulders, it enhanced Barnes's narrow frame. In silhouette he looked positively angular, puissant—an up-and-coming young exec. Also, Barnes's posture, which was ill-suited to loose-fitting clothes—he was perpetually leaning forward at a five-degree angle as if yoked to some invisible burden—was genuinely becoming in his well-tailored Universal Blue. It gave him an aura of charged potency.

"How do I look?"

"Perfect. Like a young executive. Even your shoes are well shined. Here, I bought you this." She handed Barnes a small present.

"What's this?"

"You'll see."

Barnes undid the ribbon and opened the box. Inside was a leather-bound notebook.

"Thanks," Barnes said, genuinely touched.

"In case you get a real job while you're working down there."

"That's the hope," he said. "My strategy is: This is just a stepping-stone. Something to get me in the door of the building. Once I get a foothold, who knows what may happen."

"Anything," she said.

"Yes, for sure. Anything. One of these days I'll even have an office job. I promise you."

"I'm so excited."

"My luck is bound to turn sooner or later. In the meantime . . ."

"In the meantime you have this job. It's a step in the right direction."

"I agree."

Barnes slipped the notebook inside his suit jacket and gave her a hug. "Thank you for bearing with me. It's only a bad spell. It will pass."

Just then Tom knocked on the door. He was holding a coffee mug.

"Good luck," Tom said, holding his free hand out. "Knock 'em dead, okay?"

"Thanks, Tom. Thanks for everything. The self-help manuals. The support. Sticking by me in my hour of darkness. I owe you."

"It was only a half hour of darkness. Don't kid yourself. By the way, you look great in your suit. Maybe they'll give you a promotion on your first day."

"Well, I'm hoping for a fresh start."

"Here's hoping," Tom said, tipping his coffee mug. Mia stood on her toes to give him a kiss, and Barnes was off.

8

The bus trip to the Loop was most unpleasant, and Barnes regretted almost immediately not taking a cab, or even more, not driving. He drove a 1972 six-cylinder AMC Hornet that he'd inherited from a former roommate of his, who had given him the car in lieu of six months' rent. The car shook and rattled terribly over forty mph, it lost power on hills, stalled at stoplights, and got awful gas mileage, but Barnes liked to brag it had good air-conditioning and an FM radio that worked as long as you didn't have the rear-window defroster on.

The bus was crowded, standing room only, and he clung apelike from a bar that hung down from the ceiling. It was humiliating to be packed in with all these people; it reminded him of a cattle car or worse, a sardine can, or worse . . . but what could be worse than this? The bus was hot, stultifying. What's more he was in his best suit. He wiped a bead of sweat. As the bus drove off, he scanned the seats to see if there were any attractive females on board and he thought there might be one up front, but it was too difficult to tell because there were too many people between him and her. A short squat man who wore heavy glasses and clutched a newspaper stood next to him, mumbling under his breath. Was he crazy? Barnes wondered. It seemed likely, and his breath stank of fish—sardines. When the bus lurched into traffic, the squat man slammed into Barnes, driving his elbows into Barnes's kidneys. Barnes winced and tried to remain calm. The bus turned left then right, and every time it hit a bump Barnes felt an elbow. He looked at his watch and estimated a half hour more of this. Barnes grew concerned that the man's fishy smell would rub off—which in turn could impact his first day on the job. First impressions are lasting impressions, he thought. The world seemed unfairly poised against him. The bus stopped at a library, and the woman Barnes thought might be pretty got off. He lowered his head to peer out the window to get a better glimpse and discovered, to his horror, it was a man wearing a ponytail.

"Do you mind?" Barnes asked, pushing the guy next to him, knocking him off-balance so that he fell and brought two other people down with him. Cups flew, burning people in the seats with hot coffee. This started a row. There was pushing and shoving. Somebody grabbed Barnes in a headlock, brought him down to the ground, and another person began kicking him in the side for good measure.

"You goddamned bastard!" somebody screamed. Another woman yelled, "Stop it! I've got a baby in my arms." And yet another voice screamed, "I'll sue!"

The driver of the bus, who was large as a linebacker,

got up off his seat and pushed his way through the crowd. When he came to Barnes sprawled out across the floor, he grabbed him by the legs, directed the man who smelled like sardines to give a hand, and together they pitched him, bodily, onto the side of the road. His briefcase came flying after him. Barnes lay there and watched while the bus resumed speed and merged back into traffic without him.

9

He arrived at the building on LaSalle Street bloodied, dirtied, and out of breath. Barnes felt as if he'd already lost the battle. Of all places to show up looking like you just got beat up on the roadside. He saw a group of men in suits walking toward him and he quickly dodged out of their way. Who am I fooling? he thought. To think I can be one of them. Look at me. I'm a wreck. Take it as a sign, he thought. He found a small bathroom in the dark basement, jimmied it open with a comb that was in his pocket, and washed himself off. He was scuffed up, bruised; his elbow hurt. He looked at his watch: he was just on time. He took a swipe at his hair with the comb and went to work.

The shop only had room enough for two desks—one for Charles Augustus Coneybeare and one presumably for Barnes. He set his briefcase on the desk, felt inside his coat jacket for his new leather-bound notebook, and discovered it was gone. It must have fallen out of his pocket in the ruckus. He couldn't believe his luck. He looked around the small office, getting his bearings, and was shocked, dumbfounded. He couldn't believe that of all places, he had suddenly ended up here. This is worse than ground level. It's the tar pit. He felt like a jackass, a moron, an idiot. Is this crazy, coming in here as if I were some sort of executive? Who am I fooling? And then he thought, It's desperation making me do this. He remembered belatedly one of his pamphlets that argued: "And never! Never ever ever *ever* act out of desperation! It only leads to no good!" Too late now, Barnes thought. I'm here. I'm desperate. No turning back.

On each desk was an ancient black phone, a stack of thumb-smudged annual parts manuals, and a cup that held miscellaneous paper clips. An old wooden coat-tree, circa 1950, with tarnished brass hooks was topped with a dusty chapeau and pushed into the corner of the shop. Above Coneybeare's desk were yellowing *National Geographic* photos of polar bears cutely recumbent on ice floes. A caption in blue letters read: "Chill Out." No nudies, Barnes thought with some surprise, and then, turning, he noticed, on the wall just behind the coat-tree, a gilt-framed Vargas pinup. She was a pink-skinned beauty in a leopard swimsuit bottom. Her smooth modest breasts were all milky nostalgia, and for a moment Barnes thought he might be in love, though with what he couldn't quite say.

Barnes stood in the cramped, oleaginous space and, despite the influence of the Vargas girl, he felt a rising impulse to turn tail. It's not too late. I suppose I could leave before I even get started. What would Mia do? he wondered. Certainly she wouldn't stoop to a job like this.

Startling him, one of the black phones rang. He didn't know whether to pick it up or let it lie like a sleeping dog.

He decided on the latter course of action, and it was then, caught in the act of standing around on the job, when Coneybeare silently entered the office. He wore a green canvas jumpsuit, a tool belt from which were slung one pair of chrome channel lock pliers, a screwdriver, and something Barnes hadn't seen since his early youth: a white rabbit's foot for good luck. A pair of grimy safety goggles dangled from Coneybeare's neck, and on his long narrow feet he wore heavy black boots that looked like they'd been pulled off a WWII paratrooper. Whereas Barnes had spent most his life in a sort of limbo between thought and action, mind and body, Coneybeare, by contrast, seemed a man of electrified head-to-toe action. He pushed into the room and with unbelievable manual dexterity and an infinitely graceful gesture picked up the phone. In warm cello tones, he quietly conducted business with what appeared to be a frantic woman trapped in an elevator between the twenty-ninth and twenty-eighth floors. In between his conversation with the woman, Coneybeare paused, cupped the receiver, and related to Barnes what was taking place.

"A frantic female . . . god . . . yes, ma'am . . . okay . . . yes . . . yes," Coneybeare said in warm cello tones. "But are you going up or down? . . . Up . . . or down, lady," he reiterated after a pause. "Up or down? . . . Down! . . . thank you . . . I get this all the time," he said to Barnes. "Yes, ma'am," he said, converting his tone to a harsh nasal. "Just lay off the red button . . . I said just lay off . . . just . . . yes, we'll be right . . . yes . . . I understand that . . . but whatever you do don't press the . . . okay? . . . yes . . . don't worry . . . we *will* be right there."

Coneybeare slammed down the phone. His voice decompressed to a slack bassoon. "Oh Jesus . . . I'm getting too old for this." He pulled a Salem from his front pocket and in a fluid gesture popped open a brass Zippo. "Frantic females!" Coneybeare said, exhaling smoke. "I avoid them, if I can, like the plague . . . absolutely frantic . . . something about the female voice raising an alarm that always gets me. . . . I need a drink. . . . Do you drink . . . or smoke . . . or are you a teetotaler? . . . or—no . . . thank god. . . . I was worried there for a second. I thought I was going to have to fire you for insubordination."

Barnes took the proffered Salem. He looked at his watch and saw it was eleven minutes to eight—still too early for booze. Nevertheless he wasn't going to say no to his new boss.

Coneybeare reached into the top drawer of his desk and pulled out a half-finished pint of whiskey. He cleaned two glasses by blowing the dust off them.

"You know, the thing about this job, Barnes . . ." He poured two fingers into each glass, then added an extra finger to his own. "The thing—and I'm telling you . . . I mean it's one of the things that people . . . that the people in this office building . . . I mean I'm talking mainly about the suits . . . but I'm also talking about the skirts as well . . . but when I first started in this business it was mainly just suits . . . but now you have women coming in from the . . . they come in from all over. . . . They take the train in from the suburbs . . . I mean they come to these huge office buildings, and because they come from the suburbs— well they're just not used to . . . they don't understand elevators . . . that elevators have a . . . I mean elevators are people, too. . . . And I know you think that sounds crazy . . . but let me tell you the bank of elevators we have in this building . . . if they could only tell the stories of what goes on inside. . . . But you know people don't understand that about elevators . . . I mean those from the . . . the ones that come in on the trains . . . But a person who is born in the city . . . who is born and raised in the city . . . I mean, I for one grew up in a high-rise . . . so elevators . . . I mean, I knew all about them ever since I was a . . .

"Hell, I'll tell you a funny story . . . when we were kids we used to play around the elevator shafts . . . and, well, the thing about kids—and thank god we don't have no children in this building—but the thing about kids is they love a deep elevator shaft . . . we'd drop all sorts of things down these shafts . . . pennies . . . and count as they fell and well, one day . . . I don't know maybe I was nine or something like that, but one day . . . these two brothers and me are standing near the elevator shaft pretending . . . I mean we're playing this game called blindman leap . . . and the object is to try to scare the other people . . . but we were playing blindman leap . . . and one brother says something offensive to the other . . . and before I know it there's a tussle, and the first brother he's falling down the elevator shaft with his hands out by his side and flapping . . . I mean here's this little boy . . . but I was a little boy, too . . . I mean at the time . . . but here he is falling forty-something stories . . . and he's flapping his arms because he thinks maybe he can fly . . . but when he hits the ground you know what this other one does . . . you'll get a kick out of this . . . but he starts laughing . . . I mean that's kids for you." Coneybeare lifted his drink. "Cheers," he said.

"Cheers," Barnes said. "But are we going to save her?"

"Ah, let her sit there for a while . . . let her reflect, if you will, on the power of the . . . of the Elevator Commission . . . of the uh . . . we will it so be it . . . that power . . . and if we don't will it . . . look what happens . . . everything goes to hell. . . . But I was telling you, the thing about executives is they just don't realize how hellish this job can be sometimes. . . . I mean when the elevator is running okay everything is fine, fine . . . but as soon as it malfunctions all hell breaks loose . . . and then who's there to make things work again? . . ." Coneybeare lifted a wry brow and stared from beneath it. "See it all the time, especially with these old elevators." Coneybeare chuckled under his breath, "We're the guys at the bottom of the world . . . we're the guys that really make things work . . . not them. . . . Once freed a guy . . . an executive, chrissake, who was so panicked when the elevator broke down that he shat in his pants and all over the floor . . . ha-ha-ha . . . waiting for us to come to the rescue . . . and who . . . who I ask you . . . do you think had to clean it up?"

"You?" Barnes suggested.

"Me!" Coneybeare chuckled. "Try your predecessor."

This fact shook Barnes up. He wondered if, called upon, he'd be able to clean executive shit off an elevator floor.

"And let me tell you . . . these executives who ride up and down the elevator all day . . ."

"Yes," Barnes said.

"Don't think their shit don't stink."

Barnes attempted a modest smile.

"Do you think you can handle such a thing?" Coneybeare asked.

"I don't know?"

"I mean if called upon to clean up shit or vomit in the elevator, do you think you'd be able to handle it?"

Barnes thought about it a moment. He wondered how he had gotten himself into this position: it was either clean up vomit or go back to reading his pamphlets and scrounging for a job. He tried to think positively.

"Yes, I think so."

"You better think so . . . because . . . because that's what you've just hired on for . . . ha-ha, ha-ha." Coneybeare's voice turned bitter. "Jesus, I hope you're an improvement over my last hire . . . completely useless . . . I should have seen it at the time, but I was blinded I suppose . . . we all have our . . . have . . . we all have our blind spots . . . yes, even I have been known to lapse from time to time and with him I made a mistake. . . . He fancied himself a mechanic." Coneybeare burst out laughing. "Can you believe it, a mechanic!"

Barnes tried to laugh along, but it was a vain attempt.

"He showed up his first day of work . . . with a tool belt around his waist. He stepped into this office and caught me by surprise. . . . I didn't want a mechanic—he called himself a craftsman—I wanted a cleanup man . . . but he proved to be neither. . . . His tool belt was just like mine . . . in fact this is his tool belt . . . even this rabbit's foot belonged to him . . . I forced him to give it over to me . . . but he didn't like that . . . broke his spirit taking it away

from him like that . . . forced him to quit . . . he was a fool
. . . there was no talking sense to him. . . . I later saw him
panhandling on the street . . . and I told him th' day he
refused one of my orders, 'Listen to me, or a man of your
caliber . . . or someone with skills like yours will end up
on the street . . . nobody'll take someone like you. . . .' And
there he was as I predicted . . . out on the street . . . boy did
I get a belly laugh out of that. . . . Next I heard he ended
up confined in a criminal asylum. . . . But why I ever hired
that guy . . . blind spot I suppose . . . we all have them . . .
we all act against our better judgment, once in a while . . .
even the best of us. . . . But listen, Barnes, we're gonna have
to do something about that suit. . . . Can't stand to see you
standing around looking like a young executive . . . it hurts
my eyes and it's an affront . . . it's an affront, I say, to the
commission that you've signed on to represent. . . . You're
an elevator man now . . . a working stiff doing something
real. Count your blessings! They—those suits—they may
not notice us, but don't feel bad . . . you'll see . . . after a
while you won't notice them either! Though we work in
the shadows or the margins or the what have you . . . we
do very important work. . . . Over there's your uniform . . .
in that box . . . try it on . . . see if it fits . . . that, too, by the
way, belonged to your predecessor . . . and also get rid of
the shoes . . . we accept nothing but steel-toed boots on
this job."

10

In the box was a green jumpsuit, crumpled, grease-stained. It smelled like sweat. Barnes looked at the jumpsuit, then thought about the fresh starched shirt and the moderately new Universal Blue suit he currently had on. This morning, before leaving for work, he had dressed himself with care—with love!—and first there was the disaster roadside that abraded the suit fabric along the knee, the elbow, and the derrière—and now there was this: he had to relinquish his suit and briefcase for somebody else's clothes. It was disgusting and alienating to say the least.

"Is this it?" Barnes said, lifting the green jumpsuit as if it were a dead rat he held by the tail.

"That's it exactly," Coneybeare said. "Now why don't you throw it on so we can go get this woman. . . . I'm afraid she may be a screamer . . . if you know what I mean. . . ."

Barnes pulled the jumpsuit out of the box. "And where would you like me to change?"

"Change here chrissake . . . where do you think? . . . This

office is your home as much as mine . . . feel free . . . go right ahead . . . nobody will see you but me . . . and her." Coneybeare directed his eyes to the Vargas girl, whose line of sight was all but obscured by the 1950s coat-tree.

Barnes peeled off his Universal Blue suit jacket, unloosened his tie, and carefully unbuttoned his starched white shirt; he slipped off his polished wing tips, then turned his backside to long-limbed Coneybeare—who, by the way, was pouring himself two more fingers of whiskey—and faced the pink-skinned Vargas girl. For a moment he wished she were the only person in the office with him, but alas, it was only a wish. He shyly pulled off his pants, one leg at a time, and before he knew it, he was nude but for his tighty-whities. In fact, Barnes felt worse than nude, he felt naked, somehow violated by the greasy lightbulb that stared ominously from its exposed ceiling socket. Barnes, feeling as mournful as Job, folded his clothes carefully and set them aside on what, he presumed, was his desk. Then, with his right toe pointed earthward, he gingerly slipped on the soiled jumpsuit. Poor other guy, Barnes thought. He was probably fired for doing his job but being unable to please this Coneybeare, who's as nutty as a pecan pie. Obviously he's the sort that relishes the absolute power he holds over the staff here. How did I end up in this situation? Barnes felt at the end of his rope. Stupid to have ended up here, he thought. After receiving a BA from a major institution, you would have thought I'd have ended up anyplace but here. And yet here I am, an absolute failure and disappointment even to myself.

The jumpsuit was baggy around his waist and loose around his chest, the pant cuffs hung below his heels, and his sleeves dangled past his thumbs. The whole jumpsuit hung so misshapenly and loosely that Barnes reckoned it'd take a whole team of tailors to size it down to his dimensions. The fabric was rough and abraded unpleasantly at the friction points: his armpits were chafed, his elbows rubbed, and his crotch itched like a bad omen. He suppressed an urge to protest the grease-stained, sweat-penetrated jumpsuit, but he merely offered instead, a mournful smile to his new boss.

"Well," he said.

"Well, nothing," Coneybeare said. He downed his whiskey, and, contrary to the law of alcohol, became less loquacious. "Throw your shoes on, and let's go get the bitch."

Coneybeare, whose own jumpsuit happened to fit like a glove, cinched his tool belt around his waist. He then pulled from a metal desk drawer gear for climbing mountains: a harness belt, a green nylon rappelling rope, two or three worn aluminum pulleys, and a bunch of steel carabiners.

"What's all that for?" Barnes asked, concerned.

"What's it look like?"

"I don't know."

"It's rappelling gear . . . is what it is . . . and I hope you know how to use it."

Barnes, who had a mad urge to scratch his itchy scrotum, thought back to the job application questionnaire and couldn't remember if one of the questions addressed the issue of mountain climbing, so he vaguely shook his head yes.

"Good," Coneybeare said brusquely. "Now's your chance to play King Kong and rescue the screaming damsel." Coneybeare handed Barnes the climbing gear. "You carry this. . . . I'm too done in from whiskey . . . also, I want to see how you perform. . . . Consider this part of your probationary period . . . now come on . . . let's march up and get her. . . ."

11

Whereas the march up the thirty-odd flights of stairs (in what was otherwise a dark, dingy, oppressively claustrophobic stairwell that had been marked "Warning: Authorized Personnel Only") seemed to progressively sober up Coneybeare, by contrast, the stairs nearly destroyed Barnes. My first day on the job, Barnes thought. This is more than I bargained for.

Barnes was a man who, for the most part, disdained exercise of even the most modest dimensions. He made exceptions when nervous energy needed to be burnt off, but by and large he viewed exercise—or rather the unnecessary expenditure of energy on useless activities— as being tantamount to a sort of treason of the soul. In other words, Barnes reasoned, there was something about exercise that dampened the efflorescence of the inner spirit—or what Barnes liked to think of as the human aura. Perhaps this dampening agent was nothing more than sweat. Nevertheless, despite the health benefits accrued by exercise—an increased life span, a more prolonged sex drive, and a shiny, more radiant complexion—Barnes preferred, instead, the soft spot on his old mauve couch and his living room window through which he might observe the passing world.

In a city of joggers, Barnes preferred to be a walker. In a city of stair climbers, he preferred to be an escalator taker. In a city of vegetarians, well, quite necessarily, he preferred to eat meat. In fact Barnes would have preferred—if only the world would have let him—to sit out of harm's way, enjoying his mild nicotian habit and cultivating his peripatetic reading of daily newspapers, magazines, and now, self-help manuals. He lived thus, if not happily, at least at a basal level of contentment versus self-loathing that he could deal with. A favorite motto of his was: No surprises. However, this new change of events—Barnes working as a common laborer on the Elevator Commission—brought on as it was by dastardly pecuniary pressures exacerbated by a self-loathing, presumably caused by low self-esteem, which in turn was related, though perhaps only tangentially, to the general anathema of having been fired from his last job, was more than Barnes could chew, at least on this, his first day on the job. In short, the verticality of his current mission— the climbing of seemingly innumerable steps—was so counter to his mode of being that it absolutely freaked him out, not to mention it nearly broke him in two; mind and body snapped just like that.

"It's ironic you'll find . . . ," Coneybeare yelled down after him, "though this is the Elevator Commission we spend most of our time climbing up and down this staircase. . . .

You'll get used to it though . . . all this walking . . . good for you . . ."

Together boss and worker marched up thirty flights of stairs. Coneybeare, for his part, banged his heavy paratrooper boots and whistled music from *The Bridge on the River Kwai*. Little did Barnes know at the time that it was the only song Coneybeare would ever whistle, and he was one of those inveterate whistlers. Barnes marched slowly behind, cursing his luck. He seemed weighed down by gravity, by weak lungs, by even weaker legs, and by his oversized jumpsuit, which fit as loosely on Barnes as it might on a coat hanger. Barnes lifted one leg after the other, often pausing for a breath, periodically noting that the next step might be his last. He wiped his hair, which was matted with perspiration, from his brow. The *thump thump* of Coneybeare's boots echoed as the gap between them receded into several flights of stairs.

Periodically he heard Coneybeare yell down in a mild irritation: "Are you coming or what . . . chrissake . . . remember this is still your probationary period. . . ."

The sheer distance that opened between them gave Barnes the illusion that instead of moving upward, he was moving downward. The illusion nauseated him, and for a moment Barnes felt he might vomit. Barnes didn't vomit. He did, however, march on.

As he walked up all those stairs Barnes was put in mind of his childhood, which had been lived on the flatlands of Iowa. His mother used to claim that there was nothing flatter in all the world than the flatlands of Iowa. (Not true, Barnes later learned. Modern topologists had discovered that Kansas—proverbially flat as a pancake—was even flatter than Iowa and, for that matter, pancakes.) On the first Saturday of each month the two of them used to stand, side by side, in the middle of the old tarred road leading out to nowhere. They would look west toward the setting sun. Out there, in the middle of the tarred road, nothing could obstruct their view. There was the vibrating atmosphere and clouds of gnats and swifts swooping around and red-winged blackbirds flying hither and thither from fence post to fence post. Barnes presumed that his mother had waited each month in the center of the road for his father to return. In fact, Barnes had so often associated looking for his father with those desolate evening strolls that he'd come to think of the setting sun as a sort of surrogate dad. Odd then that he'd forgotten she *would* meet someone out there. Forgotten until just now. Occasionally his mother would tell him to stay where he was, and off she'd walk to a stand of trees in the distance. She'd wait there and then, from a crossroad, a man would arrive. Barnes would watch the silhouette of his mom and the man as they went on talking to each other. Occasionally they would grab hold of each other's hands and periodically they would embrace. Who was he, that man? Barnes wondered. And how strange that after all these years I just now remembered him. Barnes hadn't thought of those evening walks in years. Barnes had so desperately wanted to see his dad emerge from the epicenter of the setting sun, which had appeared like a mushroom cloud on the heat-distorted horizon that he had failed to think anything of this other man who emerged from a small gravel road that led along Bottom's Creek and dead-ended at the

Jones farm. And now, walking up these stairs, it occurred to Barnes that the gentleman in question was probably one of the local farmers, probably even Blaire Jones himself—the farmer whom he, Barnes, used to shoot duck and pheasant with when he was a boy.

Another reason, perhaps, why these meetings never registered with him, is that his mom had always been so lonesome and friendless; it never occurred to him that she might be meeting this man for reasons having to do with friendship and intimacy. He remembered her now, going up the stairs, how she raised him out there along Bottom's Creek so far from any kids his own age, thereby inflicting him with the same antisocial malady that had doomed her. He hated living out there in the middle of the cornfields with the end of the earth looming as close as the edge of the yard. She always used to complain how misunderstood she was. No one appreciated her. She was smarter than she had been given credit for. How could they not see that her self-restraint was somehow related to her intelligence and to all the ideas she had bubbling just beneath the surface? She wrote poetry, for crying out loud. She filled a whole shoebox with all the poems she wrote. How many people in this world can honestly say they wrote poems as adults? Wasn't such an accomplishment an indication that she had brains, ideas? "Why then," she would ask Barnes as they sat eating breakfast or dinner at a little oak table she had pulled up next to the window, "why can't they see that I'm more than just a secretary? Why do they refuse to acknowledge that I might be able to do something more than type letters and sort papers?"

She had spent most of her adult life working for Jack and Mary Brown, the proprietors of Rural Realty. In all the years she had worked there, they never consulted her in any important decisions relating to the business. They themselves were terrible decision makers, and it was a miracle that the business had managed to survive as long as it had.

Periodically she liked to say: "If there were any competition whatsoever in this town, they would be out of business in a heartbeat." That's what she liked to say about them. That was her final epitaph on them. When her son asked her, "Well then, Mom, why don't you go see about starting your own realty business and give them a run for their money?" she was quick to point out that she didn't have the time or the extra money to earn her real estate license. "It's all I can do, managing this household by myself, you know that, and I resent you even asking me such questions. Who do you think you are talking to your mother like this? It's you, don't you see," she would say, pointing an accusing finger at him, "it's you that prevents me from going out there and making something of my life. I don't have the luxury of time or money that most people have to lavish upon myself the education I would need to start up my own business." And he would say back to her, "Well, if you don't have the time, then stop complaining and don't be surprised that they never ask you your opinion."

"Oh, they ask me my opinion, all right. They like to know what I think about this person or that person, and I'm always happy to tell them. I don't spare them the truth even though I know it's the truth they least want to hear."

"Then no wonder they never ask you your opinion. Don't you think they know how you feel about them, too?"

"Oh, how would they know?" she'd say. "They don't have a clue how I feel about them."

Her employers, whom she loathed, didn't have the courage to fire her, and she didn't have the courage to quit, so she and the Browns lived uncomfortably tied to each other. They worked together, the three of them, in the same small office, for decades. The Browns apparently didn't approve of her lifestyle: she was a single mom who failed to attend church. According to her, they treated her as if they were morally superior to her. They were churchgoing folks. Of course, she despised church. Barnes had never even stepped inside the church that everyone else in town went to. *It was stupid she stayed there working for those people. She could have done anything she wanted. She was bright. She was beautiful. Why did she stay?* he wondered. It was funny she never had any friends. He always thought his mother was an attractive woman, and Barnes remembered, as a child, feeling enormous pride in her. She loved her vegetable garden and surrounded the house with lilac bushes that bloomed so beautifully in the spring. Even now, the smell of lilacs put him in mind of his childhood home. In spring, too, he and his mom had a tradition of planting a half-dozen rows of potatoes. It was there, one day, when he was eleven or twelve, when she told him about his dad. She told him that he had been a nuclear scientist and had died as a result of radiation sickness. The story never made sense to Barnes. He even read all the literature he could get his hands on about the building of the bomb and the dropping of the bombs on Nagasaki and Hiroshima. He read the literature, looking for some clue to his father, but was never able to find any clue.

How could she have been so friendless, a woman like her? In fact it wasn't until Barnes had left Iowa for Chicago and met other people that he realized how strange it was that she had been so friendless. No one ever called to check in on her. The only people she ever talked about were the Browns, her employers. As far as he could tell the only friend she had had was that shadowy man she met at the end of the road. Did they have sex? He never knew, though in retrospect he hoped that they had. In retrospect he wished that his mom had gotten some satisfaction out of life. It made him sad beyond belief to think that she probably hadn't.

12

"Are you coming?" Coneybeare hollered.

"Yes," Barnes shouted back, "I'm coming." He clung to the railing and pulled himself up stair by stair. When he reached the thirtieth floor, Coneybeare was lying flat on his back in the stairwell, smoking a Salem.

"Are you okay, Barnes?"

"Yes."

"I hope so, because this is a very important part of the mission."

"Just let me catch my breath."

"You wanna smoke?"

"Sure." Barnes accepted the Salem, took one puff, and got incredibly buzzed.

"A long time ago . . . when I was your age . . . I had ideas I was going to be somebody. . . . I did what you're doing . . . I came down wearing a suit just like you did this morning . . . I thought I was really going to kill them. . . ."

Barnes looked at Coneybeare like he was crazy.

"If someone would have suggested that one day I'd end up running the Elevator Commission, I would have laughed in their face. . . . I wanted to be rich . . . I wanted to be powerful . . . I dreamt of being a boss in one of those glitzy boardrooms with a view high above the city . . . money, too . . . I desperately wanted to be rich . . . earning *more* than the regular guy made . . . because you see . . . living the life of a regular guy . . . didn't seem enough. . . . Of course, I *was* a regular guy . . . I was just too proud to admit it . . . I always used to say . . . you only live once . . . may as well spend your life at the top . . . that was my philosophy . . . and for a while . . . for a while I did okay for myself. . . .

"I started a small firm that specialized in training office workers to think positive . . . I eventually got into niche publishing . . . self-help manuals, that sort of thing . . . I wrote advice for all sorts of people and pioneered the use of the exclamation point. . . . My advice to you, if you ever write advice . . . use the exclamation point! Use it liberally! It works like a charm! I sold tens of thousands of these pamphlets . . . I lived like it, too . . . writing advice on success became a self-fulfilling prophecy. . . . I only had to hold up my own success as proof that my advice was sound . . . but to be honest with you . . . I scribbled down whatever came to mind and published it. . . . I raised questions like . . . which way is up? . . . Silly stuff, really . . . the timeworn bromides were my stock in trade. . . . Let me tell you . . . we eventually had a large office in a building like this, and I had my boardroom. . . .

"It was exhilarating . . . for a while . . . but I could never shake the feeling it wasn't what I thought it should be . . . having one of those offices . . . the successful business . . . the cash . . . doling out nonsense pitched as advice to a bunch of suckers desperate to get ahead . . . it all seemed like . . . I don't know. . . . Then one day I was leaving the office at 9:00 p.m. . . . What the hell was I doing at the office at 9:00 p.m.? . . . But that was my life . . . I practically lived in the office . . . that night I got on the elevator at the seventy-second floor . . . the doors closed . . . I waited for the elevator to move and when it didn't move . . . I pushed the Open button . . . that didn't work. . . . I waited a moment or two, figuring that if I just waited then the mechanical business would work itself out and I'd be able to get on my way . . . go home and get some dinner. . . . I pushed every button on the panel and when that failed I pulled the Emergency button. . . . Nothing happened, then the lights went out in the elevator and I was stuck there in the dark. . . .

"A lot of things go through your head when you're stuck in an elevator at that time of night . . . the building all but empty . . . the small dark space closing in around you . . . I hate small spaces . . . I have an irrational fear of them . . . stuck in the elevator that night I literally thought—this is the crazy thing—I literally thought I was going to die . . . suffocate or something . . . I had a panic attack. . . . I've never had one of those before . . . but something about being powerless in a dark elevator . . . it puts you in mind of the grave. . . . Here I was all my life running my own little business . . . top of the world . . . all my life . . . everything was always under control . . . I'm the most invulnerable man in the world . . . but here was a situation completely out of my control. . . . The key thing I realized all of a sudden . . . was learning how to manage my fear of being stuck in the elevator . . . I realized that it was only a matter of time before someone came to my aid . . . at the latest it would be morning . . . someone would try to get on this elevator and find out it wasn't working . . . they'd contact a mechanic and I'd be free. . . . So I tried all the buttons again, hoping the Emergency button would work. . . . When all that failed . . . I took my suit jacket off . . . rolled it up in a ball . . . and lay down with my head on it like a pillow. . . .

"The things I dreamt of that night . . . locked up in the elevator . . . let me tell you . . . I dreamt that I had it all wrong . . . that I had come to a fork in the road . . . one road led to a life of fortune . . . the other road led . . . who knows where it led? . . . The sign didn't say. . . . I took the wrong road . . . the one that led to fortune. . . . In my dream I had a chance to retrace my steps and try the other route . . . I had no idea where that route would take me . . . but I followed it and I don't remember anything about that strange new road, only that I felt happy while walking down it. . . .

"In the morning at 7:00 a.m. sharp the lights turned on in the elevator . . . I felt it *bump bump*, and then quietly it descended on its cables to the lobby. . . . It was the most exhilarating experience . . . and when the doors opened at the lobby . . . this older gentleman . . . in a jumpsuit with channel locks greeted me. . . . He smiled at me and said, 'Are you okay, sir? . . . Sorry about any inconvenience. . . . How long you been stuck there?' . . . I was so thrilled to be rescued I gave him a hug . . . I was a changed man even though . . . even though . . . we don't always realize we are changed when the change happens. . . .

"I wandered around awhile after that experience feeling

disconnected . . . out of sorts . . . I was grumpy at work. . . .
I was depressed. . . . I didn't know how to get out of my
head the sense that I had charted the wrong direction. . . .
Wealth . . . who needs wealth? . . . Chrissakes, the most
overrated thing in the world . . . money and the way we
all kill ourselves for it. . . . Then one day it occurred to me
I absolutely had to change my life. . . . *Change your life!*
Change your life! . . . It was the philosophy that undergirded
my advice . . . I even wrote a pamphlet with 'Change Your
Life' in the title . . . but I myself had never taken the advice
seriously . . . and I saw it was time to do so . . . nothing
short of an identity change would do. . . .

"I remembered playing around with elevators as a kid
and I admit I had a mild fascination for the machines . . .
also what if I were to join the Elevator Commission and
rescue someone just as I had been rescued? . . . What if it
were me who had come to the aid of someone stuck in the
elevator all night . . . lowered them down to the lobby . . .
then greeted them inquiring after their health? . . . It seemed
a salubrious thing to do . . . and that's the thing . . . it would
be about doing. . . . So much of what I did . . . concocting
fake fraudulent advice . . . seemed empty . . . devoid of
action. . . . So what I did was I contacted the guy in the
jumpsuit who saved me . . . his name was Smitty Smith . . . a
real and authentic gentleman . . . let me tell you . . . and if the
people applying for elevator jobs these days had one-tenth
of Smitty's stature . . . the world would be a better place. . . .

"He taught me everything I know about this business
. . . most of all he taught me how to enjoy it . . . I learned
this by watching him . . . couldn't stop watching that guy

. . . and you know it wears off on you. . . . I never regretted what I did . . . tossing it all in like that . . . most people would say I was crazy giving all that up for a job like this . . . but . . . but . . . this has been the best, most enjoyable job I've ever had. . . . Once in a while I'll see one of my old colleagues running around like a chicken with his head cut off . . . running around with those foolish advice brochures . . . I always pity them . . . I often see my old colleagues running around . . . their health gone to hell from stress . . . interesting thing . . . they walk right on past me not even noticing or recognizing who I am . . . that it was me . . . *me* . . . goddamn it . . . who started that business from which they now earn their living, and hell they don't even notice me. . . . Have you caught your breath? . . . Are you ready to go?"

Barnes couldn't decide whether he was hallucinating the story Coneybeare just told him or not. He was too worn out and anxious to protest. His legs were radiating with pain. His calves and shins were tight and cramping. His lower back hurt.

"So let me ask you this."

"Shoot," Coneybeare said.

"Have you ever heard of this advice pamphlet: *Downward, Downward You Go, Which Way Is Up Nobody Knows*?"

"Of course I have, Barnes . . . of course I have . . . it was I . . . I who wrote it."

"Then you remember this advice: 'Redefine your idea of success! Think downward!'"

"Of course. . . . I wrote that when I was getting out of

the business. . . . I was already working part-time on the Elevator Commission. . . . You've heard of it. . . . How have you heard of it?"

Barnes hated to admit it, but he did anyway: "It was advice that made a difference." Barnes looked Coneybeare in the eye, and Coneybeare returned the look, raising his brows, skeptically, trying to figure out if Barnes was for real or not.

"Barnes . . . you hang by me and I guarantee you you'll be fine. . . . All right, let's do it . . . let's go and rescue the dame . . . before she gets all crazy on us. . . ."

Coneybeare didn't put his cigarette out. He merely let it slip from between his long fingers, and it fell down the space between the stairs. Barnes watched, dismayed at the distance, as the red ember disappeared in darkness, and then, like Coneybeare, he did the same, dropping his cigarette and counting one one thousand, two one thousand as it fell, a disappearing red dot, into the darkness below.

13

Coneybeare kicked the stairwell door open and stepped into the long, well-lit tile corridor that led to the elevator. Barnes walked down the long corridor, bringing up the rear. When Coneybeare got to the elevator doors, he pulled a key from his pocket, inserted it into a lock, and the elevator doors automatically popped open. He turned and flagged Barnes over.

"Hurry up, Barnes . . . I was right . . . ha-ha . . . she's a screamer."

Barnes did his best to hurry up. He could hear the woman whimpering. When he arrived at the elevator, he caught a whiff of Coneybeare, and he discovered that his boss had a bad case of body odor.

"Come on, Barnes. Bring that climbing gear over here . . . chrissakes . . . look smart . . . don't make me regret hiring you. . . . Now what I want to do is rig you up so you can go down there and save this broad . . . chrissakes, she screams."

Barnes could hear the woman's dulcet whimpering tones rising in the elevator shaft. There was a certain sweetness to them that touched his heart.

"What do you want me to do?" Barnes asked.

"Just put the harness on."

"And how?"

"Here . . . like this . . . let me show you."

Coneybeare directed Barnes in the fine points of cinching his harness. Then Coneybeare hooked one of the worn aluminum pulleys to the harness belt; he reached for a hook near one of the side cables that hung down in the elevator shaft, and hooked a carabiner there. Coneybeare moved rapidly, gracefully. He strung the green nylon rope through both the carabiner and the pulley and secured one end to a bolt that was located on the wall of the elevator shaft. He strung the other end through a clamping device that was attached to the harness.

"This way," Coneybeare explained, "if you accidentally let go of the rope . . . which I guarantee you'll do on your first try . . . this ratcheting device . . . if it holds . . . will keep you from disappearing . . . like that kid I knew . . . so long ago . . . down the elevator shaft."

Coneybeare removed the grimy goggles that were slung around his neck and handed them to Barnes.

"Here, put these on . . . just in case."

"Just in case what?"

"Just in case you need them . . . chrissakes . . . you never know with these elevators what might fall into your eyes."

Barnes reluctantly put the goggles on, complained vaguely that he couldn't see through them, then thinking better of it, pushed them back on Coneybeare. "I don't want these."

"You have to . . . it's code."

"I don't care about code. I'm not wearing them."

"Suit yourself." Coneybeare snatched them back, then peered down the shaft. "Okay, Barnes . . . it's not as far as it seems . . . it's only two stories . . . twenty-five feet . . . I'd have gotten you closer, but the doors on twenty-nine always jam when the elevators go out. . . . Blame it on the management . . . cheap bastards . . . and what comes of their cheapness? . . . Let me tell you . . . our necks . . . it's always our necks on the chopping block, with no margin for error. . . . Now the thing you have to remember . . . whatever you do . . . is don't panic. . . . You'll fall fast . . . don't worry about that. . . . Look, you can control your fall by applying pressure with your hands to the rope just beneath this pulley . . . see what I'm saying . . . here . . . you might want to use these gloves . . . but maybe not . . . you seem kinda finicky. . . . A word of warning . . . when you approach the top of the elevator car . . . just avoid the left-top panel. . . . See it there . . . if that breaks from your weight, we'll never be able to replace it . . . that's a genu-wine art deco hood, if you know what I mean. . . . Also . . . there's an electrical switch just below that panel . . . if you were to break through the panel you might get electrocuted . . . and you don't want that to happen to you do you?" Coneybeare chuckled. "Ready to go, champ?"

"I don't know," Barnes said. He was humbled. He'd never been asked to save somebody before. Particularly he'd never been asked to risk his life saving somebody else's. In all his years of living, this was a circumstance he'd never been prepared for. He always imagined that other people would step up to do the saving, not him. He reminded himself that there were worse things to do in life than to be a hero who had rescued a trapped damsel from a stuck elevator. It's just this wasn't how he wanted to do it. In theory, he thought, I'd love to save this woman, but practically speaking I don't want to risk my life doing it. I'd rather preserve my own life than save hers. In fact, I want her life preserved as well, I'd just rather someone other than me step forward and take the risk of life or limb, not me. Was he being selfish? Maybe he was. The self-preservation instinct was strong in him. There were higher things he could be called upon to do for which the sacrifice of limb or life wouldn't be too great. He thought of his imaginary dad sent in the wake of some atomic holocaust to assess the human toll. He imagined working such a mission only to die an excruciating death of radiation poisoning, leaving wife and child to fend for themselves. He thought of the urn containing his old man's ashes. Or did the urn indeed contain his mother's dog's ashes? It bothered him that he didn't know whose ashes they were. He wished retrospectively that he hadn't sent them along with his mother to the tomb. But had he not sent them to the grave with her, he would have had to do something else respectful with them. It was worse to honor the ashes as if they belonged to his dad when in fact they may have only been the ashes of a dog. That was Barnes's thinking anyway, and that's why he had decided to put the ashes in the casket with his mother: the secret and bearer of it forever linked and discharged into the fading mists of memory.

Coneybeare looked at his watch. "She's probably a young lady down there . . . judging from the sounds of her . . .

what was I saying about these women coming in from the suburbs not knowing the first thing about elevators . . . not realizing that at heart these little boxes are living creatures with souls of their own? . . . How long's she been down there? . . . Forty-five minutes . . . fifty at the most. . . . Listen, that's pretty good reaction time around here . . . in other words . . . ," Coneybeare said, "we're doing pretty good today . . . be proud of yourself. . . . Here's the key to the elevator hood . . . now look when you get down there . . . just plug this baby in . . . give it a clockwise crank . . . and the hood should pop right open for you . . . then you can shimmy your way into the compartment. . . . Use this round key here to lower the elevator to the next floor . . . just give it a half turn counterclockwise when you insert it . . . if it doesn't work . . . it doesn't work . . . what can I say? . . . That's working with old elevators . . . don't worry though, because you can bring her out the way you came . . . if that happens, I'll be up here guiding you through the steps . . . everything clear?"

Barnes nodded yes, even though he only had a very faint idea of what was required of him—and the largest portion of that idea was to jump.

"Good . . . now why don't you just stand here on the edge, and when you're ready to go . . . go . . . oh, and here . . . take this for good measure. . . ." Coneybeare removed the white rabbit's foot from his belt loop and attached it to Barnes's belt loop.

"Take it back," Barnes said bravely. "I don't need it. I'm not superstitious."

To which Coneybeare snorted, "T'hell you're not . . .

now don't be silly . . . wear it as some sort of protectorate if nothing else . . . what the hell. . . ."

"All right, then," Barnes said. He attached the rabbit's foot as directed, only to buy time. He paused, took a breath, and looked down at his hands. Can I do this? he wondered. Then he stepped up to the edge of the elevator shaft and stared down. His insides buoyed as he felt a quick flash of vertigo. Barnes tried to compose himself. He was cinched in, after all, with the harness belt around his waist, and the ropes all appeared to be fastened properly, and, as Coneybeare had pointed out, if all went wrong—and what were the chances of that happening?—it was only a two-story fall followed at most by a crash landing onto the top of the elevator. If he crashed on the wrong side of the elevator hood, well then, he might get electrocuted, but what were the chances of that happening? After all, nobody gets electrocuted these days.

Nevertheless, as Barnes stood there, he tried to remember if he knew anyone who'd ever been electrocuted. He remembered a story he'd heard only a handful of years ago about an old Iowa classmate who'd been killed by electric voltage. His ex-classmate and a handful of friends (dropouts all of them) had been partying in a train yard, the story went, when this one climbed up an idle train car and, desiring to swing from a low-hanging high-tension wire overhead, had taken a flying leap for it. His arms extended into the air, but he didn't. His foot had caught hold of the train top, and he tumbled forward. To break his fall, he reached and just caught hold of the high-tension wire. Therewith, he was socked with ten thousand volts and died. Apparently, or so the story went, the electricity was powerful enough to blow his arms and head right off. Barnes remembered being astonished when he heard this story, but not saddened. The schoolmate had been a bully, and Barnes, who in his youth had been occasional fodder for bullies, necessarily disdained the type. What's more, he later learned that they had all been high on PCP. Served him right, Barnes thought.

Barnes peered down the shaft and heard the whimpering woman's cries.

"Come on . . . let's go already . . ."

"I'm preparing myself," Barnes said diffidently.

"Well stop preparing . . . she's been down there long enough. . . ."

"Look, this could be life or death," Barnes said.

"Look . . . it could be fired and out on your ass . . . now jump!"

Barnes looked at Coneybeare. He was appalled. "All right. Just let me catch my breath."

Barnes tried to catch his breath but found himself hyperventilating. He looked to make sure his own feet were clear of any snags. Better that the high voltage leap of his classmate should function as a lesson. Just then, Barnes did what he thought he'd never be able to do: judging that he had clearance, he jumped. Why not? he thought. It was either jump or be fired. Midair, he remembered being saddened by the desperate dialectic of this choice: fork left or fork right, and the consequences, though different in the details, were invariably tragic in the wash.

As Barnes attempted to scale the air, he heard Coneybeare's retrospective voice, this time squelched in alarm, echoing after him: "The rope ... don't forget to grab hold of the rope. . . ."

14

Barnes fell through the space that was the elevator shaft, but more importantly, he fell through time. Whereas life, as a rule, is dominated by the tedium of medium time; Barnes's fall through the elevator consisted only of slow and fast time. The first moments, midair, before tension caught in the harness belt, Barnes experienced slow time. It seemed to him as if he were hanging there in midspace forever. Barnes became perceptive of details he'd never noticed before, like the rope, which swung immediately before him. It seemed to oscillate slowly in a sine wave. How does one calculate a sine wave? Barnes tried to remember; then instinctively he reached for the rope as it crested toward him. If I grab hold of the rope, I'm saved, he thought. But if I miss it, I'm doomed. Barnes contemplated for a brief moment what it might mean to be doomed. Dead, he thought. I'd be dead. And though he was too young to die, it nevertheless surprised him, as he hung midair reaching for the rope, that he was prepared to meet death calmly. Eye to eye, man to man. All stories end here. Can I deal with this? he soliloquized, and then answered, Yes, I can deal. Yes I can. His hand reached out imperceptibly as the rope swung toward him. Barnes was terrified by how calm he felt. *Shouldn't my own Being protest its demise with greater force?* The rope slipped gently into Barnes's hands, and he received it like a gift, clutching it close to his breast. He became aware of Coneybeare's voice filling the dark narrow space of the shaft. Though it was raised an octave, it nevertheless maintained a pleasant reedy tone: "Grab hold the rope . . . dummy!" There was also a strange sonar pinging sound that put Barnes in mind of depth charges. He felt merciful tension come into the rope as it took, but his hands, slippery with sweat and weak from a lifetime of idle disuse, couldn't hang on. *Were those the elevator cables twanging?*

He banged his head against something and entered fast time. His harness belt tightened around his waist, knocking the wind out of him, but the belt gave way a nanosecond later as the rope to which it was attached broke loose from its latching. Thus sliding, tumbling, caterwauling, Barnes fell. He fell and he fell and he fell. He attempted to scream in terror, but failed; then he fell and slammed into the hard hood of the elevator. His right leg punctured through, he felt a stabbing pain in his knee, his left testicle ached; something jerked his jaw back twisting his neck incontrovertibly. He felt a cut in his temple as he banged his head again. Then there was the electrocutionary shock. Had he landed on the right side or the wrong side of the hood? For a moment, Barnes thought he felt something like jackhammer voltage pulsating in his lower torso. He worried about the disfigurement such shock might bring to head and limb. His body weight, pressing on the weakened hood, caused it to give way, and with a cracking noise, he busted through.

He heard Coneybeare yell after him: "The hood . . . the hood goddamn it . . . that hood is irreplaceable . . . where are we gonna get another one? . . ."

15

Barnes thought he might be dead. If he wasn't dead he wished he were dead. Better to end it all now—before he was fired and forced to go back on the hunt for that ever elusive gumption. On the other hand, if he could only get up, maybe he could become a hero—and if a hero, what then?

Green nylon rope that had broken free from its lashings came tumbling after Barnes and piled on top of him in loopy coils. Was this the way it would end—not with a whimper but a bang? The woman whom he was here to save stood cowering in the corner. She'd been banged on the head by fiberglass fragments that had splintered off the elevator hood. A sparking electric cable swung down like a snake, narrowly missing her. There was the smell of smoke, and the confusion of noise and parts, and then this man falling through the roof—was he dead? For a moment she thought she was going to faint.

Barnes, who was probably knocked out, lay limp beneath the coils of rope. His breath came out of him in low rapid gasps. He was only vaguely aware of the woman. He thought that her shadowy Presence, rather than belonging to a woman, might belong to some sort of god or guardian angel. He imagined that she was here to punt him across the River Styx. He'd never been punted across a river before. Though once, as a kid, he had hid behind a duck blind with the local farmer and watched as green-necked mallards were stopped midflight with a 12-gauge lead shot load using #4 shot: their wings went limp and they plummeted like balled socks splashing into the marsh. He would sit white-knuckled in the bow of the boat, and the farmer would sit in the stern, and taking turns they would row sullenly to retrieve their catch.

Barnes grew vaguely aware now of his own heartbeat; it seemed a weak murmur low in his chest. Secretly he wished it would just stop. Stop, he pleaded with his heart. Stop, so that I might be able to go with this Presence. Barnes closed his eyes and tried—or rather, wished—to discover the so-called white light at the end of the tunnel, which he had been told would signify the end. He waited patiently for an outer-body experience. If he were ever going to have one, now was the time! He felt himself breaking free of his immobile mortal envelope. He thought he might be drifting, belly-up, on some sort of current—a current of peace and beatitude. Oh, how pleasant it was to be floating away, peacefully, saying farewell . . . farewell to all that—to men like clocks and to women like clocks and to the silhouettes of them like clocks, chiming time in the distance. Farewell all, farewell.

As Barnes drifted away, he caught a whiff of an acrid odor, strong as smelling salts, which seemed woven into the fabric of his canvas jumpsuit. The smell reminded him of pup tents he'd been forced, against his will, to sleep in as a scout. And always it was a terrific problem for him—how to find space all his own on the tent floor to lay his sleeping bag down so he could sleep, untouched, unfettered, the sleep of the dead. But he never could find enough space. A dirty sock was always poking in his face, and body parts pushing into his side—and the terrible smoky smell of a tent full of boys on a three-day camping trip. It made his left eyelid tremble. He reentered the sock of his body.

"Oh my god!" he heard a pleasant-sounding voice say. "I think he's dead."

Barnes thought to himself, God?

He felt the boat that he'd been drifting in jerk twice. *Thunk! Thunk!* It made a louder noise then jerked again and began a slow quiet descent on wobbly cables. I hope this doesn't mean I'm going to hell, he thought.

"Oh my god!" he heard that heavenly voice say again. "I think he's dead. And this electric wire is sparking!"

The Presence poked him with her foot to see if he'd move. But he didn't. He was inert. There was a small pool of blood forming like a halo where his head lay.

"He's dead," the Presence said aloud, loud enough for Coneybeare to hear.

"What's that, lady?" Coneybeare shouted down the shaft.

Trying to avoid the sparking wire, she peered up through the hole in the elevator hood, up into the dark shaft, up toward a trapezoid of brightness, and there she saw, framed in white light, Coneybeare's narrow foreshortened head peeking over the edge of the opening.

"Help!" she screamed. "Help! I think your friend is dead. And there's this wire thing—turn it off!"

"He's not dead!" Coneybeare screamed back. "Hell, I can see him moving!"

"He's dead! And turn this wire thing off now before it kills me!"

"Pull the red button, lady. Pull it for chrissakes!"

"Dead!" she reiterated.

"Pull the red button!"

The elevator seemed to descend more rapidly.

"Pull!"

"Dead!"

She reached for the red button and pulled, but nothing happened. The cable banged into her shoulder and she screamed in pain. "Make it stop!"

"Pull the red button," Coneybeare reiterated. It irritated him that she just couldn't pull the button.

"I am pulling it," she screamed back. "And nothing's happening."

"Then push, chrissake! Push!"

"You said pull."

"Now I say push!"

"He's dead." The live cable brushed her shoulder again, and again she yelped in pain.

"Push!" Coneybeare hollered.

She pushed the button and heard another thunk and then another, and then it seemed as if the elevator broke free of its cables and began free falling in the shaft.

"Oh my god," she screamed. "What do I do now! What

do I do! Help! It's falling faster!" The live wire bumped against her and sparked. She smelled burning.

"Jesus," Coneybeare yelled. It irritated him that this particular elevator—an elevator, by the way, that he happened to feel a particular fondness for—was being irrevocably trashed. He realized then and there that he'd made a big mistake by sending Barnes down to rescue the woman in the first place. This guy's a failure, he thought. I should have gone down there myself. The elevator was descending at the rate of one floor per ten seconds. Even if it did fall all the way down, there were safety features in place to insure that the occupants would survive. Coneybeare was irritated at the frantic female. She only seemed to make things worse by her screaming. What's more, his own colleague, a fresh hire, was lying down on the job. It was, to say the least, ignominious.

"Get up!" he screamed at Barnes. "Get up chrissakes and save the lady! Save her before she screams her head off."

16

Barnes stirred beneath the loops of nylon rope. His harness belt, cinched tight from the fall, felt like a loincloth turned vise grip. He tried to cry out in pain, but failed. What's more he lay twisted on fiberglass and metal shards that had splintered off the hood. One piece of bent metal poked uncomfortably like a spear into his side. Another piece, it seemed, poked through his feet. An electric cable (was it live?) descended from heaven knows where and dangled dangerously close to Barnes's nose. He felt entombed and stifled and desperately craved oxygen. He vainly raised the question: Why have you forsaken me?

"Call my mother," he yelled. He had meant to say: I'm dying. Please call a priest.

The shadowy Presence, who had been in a panic, rushed over to him and, disregarding the fact that it was live, pushed the cable aside.

"You're alive," the Presence said in breathless tones. "Mamma's here to help."

The elevator continued to descend, creating a vacuum. Barnes gasped for breath.

"Breathe in, breathe out," the Presence urged. She tapped his pulse rapidly with two fingers. "Come on, you can do it. One, two, three. Breathe in. You'll be all right. Mamma's here to help."

Barnes tried to follow her orders and breathed. He wheezed on the exhale and paused on the inhale, as if to collect energy. In his delirium he thought that indeed his mother was here to help. However, in all of Barnes's twenty-nine years of so-called living, his mother had never come so comfortingly close as this. She had always been cold and distant, though despite countervailing evidence, she hadn't been entirely unloving. And if Barnes was going to die (as he felt certain he would), he supposed it would be a good time to set the record straight: No, Mom hadn't been unloving at all.

As Barnes lay there, he remembered back to that time, for instance, when he got smashed by a train, and Mom, in her ironic way, had put the whole accident in perspective. They had been coming home in the late afternoon from her office in town. She liked to walk home, so as to stretch her legs from a day of sitting. Barnes would meet her after school, oftentimes on his bike, and together they would leave for home. She was a fast walker, and Barnes, who was always a slow pedaler and dawdler, would invariably fall far behind her in their homebound peregrinations.

There was that one time he had fallen so far behind his mother, that he sought to catch up by pedaling as fast as he could. She had advanced a block beyond the railroad tracks, and he was a block on the other side when a train appeared around the bend. It fascinated Barnes then and it fascinates him now that his mother had never once turned to look and see whether her son would make it across the tracks. But he made a go for it. Trying to outdo the train, he pedaled as fast as he could. The train engineer, who peeked his head out the side window, lay on his horn and flagged his hands for Barnes to get out of the way. But Barnes kept his eyes fastened on his departing mother, who, he knew, would be turning the corner any second to take Lincoln Street (which was a shortcut) home. He had meant to cry out, "Mom, wait!" but the train whistle was deafening. And he could feel the heat of the locomotive. And when his front wheel hit the track rail with a bump, it nearly caused him to fall. And still she kept walking— despite the train whistle. Thus he kept pedaling. He kept trying to catch her. And just as he made it across the last rail the locomotive caught his rear tire and flung Barnes like a rag doll out into the road of oncoming traffic, where he was nearly hit by a blue Chevrolet that came skidding to a halt. It was only then his mother turned and saw him lying there in roadside gravel. She merely chuckled, walked back to where he lay, walked as if she weren't in any great hurry, as if she wanted to make some sort of larger point, then helped him up, brushed him off, and said, "After that little stunt, kiddo, no bike for you until Christmas!"

If this isn't my mother, he wondered, then who . . . who could this Presence upon whose soft bosom I now lie be? He opened his eyes and realized that he hadn't died, that this wasn't an outer-body experience, that he was here, trapped in an elevator with a woman who was saying odd things to him.

"One, two, three. Innnn. Oooout. One, two, three. Oooout. Innnn."

"Oh my god," Barnes said, reluctant to break free from her loving embrace. With one eye open he discerned immediately that this female couldn't possibly be his mother. She was too beautiful to be his mother. The Presence had high delicate cheekbones, a thin nose, and full lips. Her teeth were set straight, probably orthodontically. (She was also probably from the suburbs, as Coneybeare had predicted.) She had a graceful neck and wore a lovely perfume. But the most striking thing about her beauty was her eyes. They were like swimming pools reflecting storm clouds. They achieved a color tone somewhere between dove gray and mouse taupe, and here and there against the pale iris were interspersed little flecks of black that somehow reminded Barnes of a scattering of birds circling through empty sky.

"Help me," he said pathetically.

"I'm doing what I can," the Presence said.

She brought his head close to her breasts. Thinking that it might do some good, she attempted to palpate his belly. (She had once aspired to be a nurse.) She waited patiently for some sort of result, then frantically pressed again. For a moment, as Barnes enjoyed her rhythmical pattings, he had a wild urge to kiss her breasts or her lips, which were also dangerously close to his own. He made a vain attempt but failed. The Presence merely smiled at his efforts then commenced to stroke the hair out of his eyes. She mused under her breath that it was going to be all right. Gratefully, he felt the vibration of her musings reverberate deep in her body cavity. I'm alive, he thought. I'm alive.

"You'll be all right," she said. "Trust me, whoever you are. Just come back to life, that's all."

Barnes stretched a trembling finger to touch her cheek and see if she were indeed real.

When his finger made contact, she mused gently, "There you are." She stroked his forehead, his cheek, and kissed him full on the lips. She kissed passionately so as to put the fire of life back in him. She pulled away only once to give him a chance for breath. Barnes lay there in her lap and felt divine, and then he kissed her back. He kissed with his eyes shut. He kissed as if he were drinking from the well of eternal life. It was, perhaps, the most blissful moment of his life. I'm alive now, he thought. I may be dead later, but this is grand. He twisted his pelvis and attempted to unloosen additional pressure building under the harness belt.

"Is that what's bothering you?" she mused quietly. She reached her hand and undid the harness belt. "That's it. There you go. You'll be all right. Yes, there." She kissed and smiled and watched Barnes's left eye flutter. Thinking that the eye flutter represented his potential passage into dark death, she said, quietly but firmly, "Don't leave me. Don't go. Not yet."

But Barnes slipped out of her hands and flipped onto all fours. He looked like a human fish whose body had gotten netted in an overlarge jumpsuit. He was buried by the nylon rope, and the cable was sparking.

"All right then, get up!" she said, astonished.

As if her words were a divine order, Barnes attempted

to fight clean of the tangles of rope and rise to his feet. He sashayed to the left, thrashed to the right, and got on both knees. He felt wobbly. Light-headed. His pant leg was in the way—though of what, he couldn't say. Leaning against the elevator wall for support, he clawed his way to bipedal position. The live electric cable dangled at his nose. With his sleeve as an insulator, he gingerly pushed it aside and shuffled to the opposite corner of the elevator. He was dismayed by the damage he'd caused but was glad to be alive. We can rebuild this, he thought. But my life . . . Just then he said, as dutifully as the present conditions would allow, "Are you okay, ma'am?" His voice croaked under pressure. He glanced quickly at her then glanced at the elevator ceiling through which he'd just fallen. He peered toward the diminishing square of light. He thought he saw the silhouetted head of Coneybeare and a coal of orange burning at the tip of his cigarette.

"Pull the red button," he heard the oboe-toned voice sing, but Barnes failed to register the command. He breathed in, looked at her once more, and asked, "Have I been electrocuted? I thought I felt a shock."

"No, darling," she said. "I don't think so. At least I didn't see any electrical sparks fly."

The expression caught Barnes's interest. He'd never been held so tenderly before in all his life, nor kissed like that. She was beautiful and he wanted to go back to the position they'd just been in.

"I was trying to give you mouth-to-mouth and bring you back to life. I read in a handbook somewhere how to do it. And look, it worked! At least I think it did. You were dead but now you are—" She looked him over carefully. His temple was bleeding. "Are you going to be okay?"

"I don't know." He wished he weren't wearing a large jumpsuit that smelled like stink. He rolled up the sleeves, then bending over, rolled up his pant cuffs. The elevator felt as claustrophobic as a tomb.

"I don't know why I'm here," he said, confused.

"I know," she offered. "You're a hero. You attempted to save my life and you almost died in the process. But I brought you back to life." She smiled at her handiwork. "You're a Lazarus returned from the dead. That's why you've come!"

"I'm a fool is more like it," Barnes said. He felt a strange connection to her. "My first day on the job and my last, I imagine."

"Mine, too," she said, "if you don't do something to stop this elevator!"

The elevator cables were rattling loudly, and the elevator car was banging against the walls as it fell through the shaft. Barnes looked up to see if Coneybeare was still there, but he wasn't—the burning coal of his cigarette was gone.

"Jesus," Barnes screamed. He jumped to action. "We gotta stop this thing."

"If you make it stop," she said, "I promise I will never, never forget you!"

Barnes, who had made a point whenever he had a chance to forget his own miserable life, was touched by the proposition. This could mean something big, he thought. Just what, he couldn't say. The red elevator button was pushed in. Thinking that it should be out, Barnes reached and pulled it, and miraculously the elevator slowed to a squeaking halt. This was followed by an earsplitting sonic alarm.

"You did it!" she screamed. "You stopped it."

She grabbed him in her arms and kissed him on the lips again.

"I think it stopped itself," Barnes hollered above the racket.

"No, you did it!" she yelled, reaching her hands around his waist. "Take some credit!"

"Listen, ma'am." He put his hands around her waist and was surprised at how warm her skin was beneath her blouse.

She placed her finger on his lip. "Sh."

"What?" he screamed.

"Sssh." She then added, "It's Marie."

"What is?"

"My name."

Barnes's lips broke free of her fingertip. "But let me just call up to my superio—"

"No," she said.

"What?"

"No, don't! Let him be." She brought her lips to his neck and kissed him. She brought them to his bare clavicle and kissed again.

"Here I feel free," she screamed.

Barnes could hardly hear what she was saying because of the alarm.

"Yes," Barnes said, touched by delirium.

Barnes reached for the switch, flicked it, and the alarm shut off. They were immediately enveloped in silence.

"You're alive," she said, in hushed intimate tones. She placed her finger over his lips. "And you're cut."

"I'm . . ." and for a moment Barnes thought she might have said he was cute—something that he had never been told before.

"Yes, you must have scraped yourself . . . you're bleeding."

"No, it's sweat." Barnes took his shirtsleeve which, having unraveled, dangled below his wrists. He attempted to wipe his brow. But the jumpsuit was polyester and lacked absorption properties.

"No, it's blood. Look at your sleeve." She pointed at the spot where he had collapsed. "Look there." She pointed at the pool of blood and the coils of rope.

She brought her lips forward and pressed them to Barnes's face. He felt her tongue push softly as she licked the blood from his temple.

Barnes was stunned.

"That's for you," she said.

Barnes grabbed her in his arms and kissed her full again on her lips, and he closed his eyes and imagined the perfect alignment of her teeth, and her beautiful dove-gray eyes.

"Thank you," Barnes said. "Thank you." He pulled away from her and looked her in the eyes. "You saved my life."

She laughed his comment away. "I told you if you stopped the elevator—"

"Right," Barnes answered again. "It's stopped."

"That if you stopped the elevator I would never forget you."

"Please," Barnes said, against his will. "Don't be silly."

"Is there something I can offer you?"

Barnes looked at her closely. He was sad to think that this moment was just a moment—though she said she wouldn't forget it yet she probably would. Nevertheless Barnes wouldn't forget it. So when she said, "Is there something I can offer you?" Barnes was too breathless to answer. He merely tried to step out of the green tangles of nylon rope that lay like reptiles at his feet.

"I don't know," he said.

"I know the higher-ups."

Barnes was still thinking of her shadowy Presence.

"I suspect you do."

"I mean, I'm connected. I know the higher-ups. If you ever need anything you can call me."

"But how—"

"Here," she said. "Wait a minute. My purse, where is it?" They both scanned the wreckage that lay on the elevator floor. "There it is." She pointed near where the puddle of blood was. "Underneath that rope."

Barnes grabbed it and handed it to her. "Here."

She rifled through her purse and pulled out a card. "My number is really easy to remember," she said. "By chance the numbers spell LOVE YOU. By chance! If they fire you for this, call me."

Barnes took the card without looking at it.

"And if they don't fire me? Can I still call you?" Barnes desperately hoped she wouldn't leave him.

"Look," she said. "We're here!"

The elevator doors sprang open and the immense lobby crowned with gold leaf domes stretched magnificently before them.

"Well, good-bye, and thanks." She paused then gave him a quick kiss. With a brief gesture she pushed his hair into place. Her gray eyes were smoldering.

"You're not leaving—"

"Yes, and thank you. And remember: I'm the one who brought you back to life."

"But hey. Wait!"

"Farewell. Farewell, whoever you are!" With that she turned, stepped into the crowded lobby, and walked rather quickly away.

17

Barnes yelled after her. "But wait a minute. My name . . . my name is Barnes!" he screamed. The sonic alarm kicked on, drowning Barnes's voice. He felt the ominous *thunk thunk*, and the elevator began, once again, a slow descent to the basement. I can't believe it. I just can't believe I could have gone. I could have left. Why didn't I just go with her? What's wrong with me? I should have gone and never looked back. I should have left this elevator. I should have walked into the lobby with her and never turned back. Barnes looked around at the wreckage strewn about the elevator. The blood. I'll probably be assigned to clean it up. What a waste. I should have left. I'm always lingering in the shadows. It's the shadows that will kill me. I was born in a shadow and I'll die in a shadow. I should have followed her into her world—a world of light without shadows!

Barnes clutched his head. Was it going to explode? He touched his lips—were they still moist from her kiss? He wished they were, but they were dry and cracked. He was dry and cracked. He couldn't believe his luck—and yet he hadn't acted on it. To have luck and fail to act on it is tantamount to not having luck at all. In fact, it was worse. Barnes thought back to his self-help manuals. They all proclaimed with compelling force the necessity of recognizing opportunity then seizing it when it struck. Metaphors were loosely dangled about: In the juvenescence of the herd comes ambition the tiger. Barnes knew that finding the inner tiger was the key to success. He had read the manuals. He understood the logic. It seemed simple. It all seemed simple on paper. Yet in real life nothing seemed more difficult for Barnes than recognizing opportunity and seizing it.

She was here. She's gone. I'm here. And look—wreckage at my feet!

Barnes pushed the Down button, and the elevator began its descent to the basement. When it finally came to a rest, Barnes was wrung out. The live cable still swung and sparked from the ceiling, and when the doors opened, Barnes avoided it like a bad omen. He nearly tripped over the pile of nylon rope and squeezed through the partially opened doors. Coneybeare was standing there with a crowbar, ready to apply any necessary torque.

"How you doing, son?"

"I'm alive," Barnes said, pushing past him. He wasn't sure whether to tell Coneybeare all that had happened.

"Yes, I see that," Coneybeare said, clanking the crowbar against the concrete floor and following after Barnes.

"At least I think I'm alive." I'll never see her again, he thought. From here on she'll exist only in my memory. He was reluctant to trust her to his already unreliable memory. He fought the urge to weep. Perhaps it's stress. He walked down a dark corridor that was lined with corkboard. He spent so much time in his own memory already. To live that way made him feel like a ghost. Old yellowed mimeographed sheets of rules and regulations pinned to the cork rustled in his wake.

"Where's the girl?"

"Gone."

"Gone! Where did she go?"

"She left. The elevator stopped at the lobby. She left then."

"Did she say anything about a lawsuit? Bitch. The way she screamed."

"No."

"Well, hopefully she'll keep quiet. That was a close one though."

"I feel like hell."

"We could have been sued, you know."

"Yes, and I could have ended up with a broken back."

"It could be worse," Coneybeare offered. "You could be dead." He hurled the crowbar into an open tool chest and followed Barnes to the office. Coneybeare was feeling triumphant. His new hire may have helped the company avoid a lawsuit. He had a wild urge for another glass of whiskey and was hoping Barnes might have a glass with him.

"Yes," Barnes said. "I could be dead." He pushed open the door to his office and flicked on the switch. Barnes paused in the dull yellow light cast from the grimy exposed bulbs above. He saw his brand-new briefcase, though empty, sitting near his desk. He saw his Universal Blue folded up on his desk, still dusty from the roadside gravel he'd been tossed into from the bus this morning. He had tenderly put his suit on while the morning was still dark. He had stood in the quiet of his apartment admiring himself in the mirror, centering himself, hoping for a grand beginning. What he'd got instead was a tumble— tossed and dumped, fallen and hurled, snared and broken. *What a fool I've been.* It seemed all for naught.

"Yes," Barnes said again, rather dubiously. "I could be dead, and that would be worse. As it is, I have nothing left in my heart—nothing but dirty hope!"

"Ah, yes," Coneybeare pointed out, his voice slackened to a pleasant hum as he pulled open the desk drawer and reached for the whiskey. "Dirty hope! But three days ago when I interviewed you for this job—you didn't even have hope!"

18

What most frustrated Barnes, especially when he was being honest with himself, was that he always seemed incapable of acting on his impulses. Inner drive, he kept saying to himself. I must learn how to get inner drive. Without it, I'm doomed to forever being who I am. It's not that Barnes didn't like being who he was. He was just concerned that if he didn't change sooner or later into something else, he might invariably be doomed.

Barnes had wanted to contact Marie immediately, but he didn't know how to go about such an elaborate business. He had her card of course, and her oddly mnemonic number: LOVE YOU. Later he often puzzled over the significance of her phone number—that its seven digits should spell out "Love you." Was she some sort of call girl or escort or prostitute or something? And what did she mean by "I know the higher-ups"? He'd accepted that proffered bit of information in his usual nonchalant manner, yet since the moment he'd heard it, it troubled him. She knows the higher-ups, but how? And why the funny phone number? Barnes had even spent one desultory Saturday afternoon (Clem quietly dozing at his side) carefully paging through all the escort ads in the yellow pages, trying to discern if she was, in fact, one of them—one of those smiling girls who posed in tuxedo bow ties and bare shoulders and who were most unfortunate to have their photographic likenesses superimposed on the dirty yellow paper of the phone book. Yet search the yellow pages though he might, he never discovered her face. This fact both troubled and elated Barnes. On the one hand he would have done anything to get his hand on Marie's simulacrum— especially a color photo so that he might study with closer scrutiny her mouse-taupe eyes with the little black spots in the irises—eyes which he had found, in real life, so unsettling. It elated him, on the other hand, that she wasn't one of them, one of those women desperate enough to willy-nilly paste their image inside something so public as the city telephone book.

At least she's not one of them, he thought. Then as an axiom, he added, She's probably too classy for that. Indeed his overwhelming impression of her—that is, his most abiding mental image of her—wasn't the Marie he encountered when he first came to consciousness in the elevator lying beneath the coils of nylon rope, the Marie of the shadowy Presence. No, the most lasting image he had had of Marie was of her stepping off the elevator and turning around and with the briefest of smiles saying, "Farewell. Farewell, whoever you are." To exit as such (especially after a traumatic elevator experience) required a level of personal esteem and charisma that Barnes had heretofore been unacquainted with—a level of charm to which he suddenly aspired. She must be royalty, descended from a clan who never had to grovel. Without knowing it, Barnes desperately wanted her, whoever she was, the moment she disappeared around the corner and off toward wherever it was she went, to the higher-ups perhaps. In fact he longed for Marie so achingly that he was loath to jinx his chances by picking up the phone, dialing those seven digits, and saying as bravely as possible when a female voice answered the phone, "Hello, this is Barnes. I rescued you the other day. Remember? And you are, I presume, Marie. And if so, you wouldn't want to see me again, would you?"

"No, I wouldn't want to see you, dear fellow. But thank you for saving my life."

Barnes made a mental note to improve his introduction. He ran through a couple of variations: Hi, this is Barnes—I want to get together with you. . . . Hi, this is the elevator guy. I would like, if possible, to see you at your earliest possible convenience. . . . Hi, remember me? You said you knew the higher-ups in this building. Well, I desperately want to. . . . Barnes wondered why he was being so pusillanimous. Surely she had given him her calling card because she had hoped he would use it. But she said to use it only if he got fired. And what were the chances of that happening? Barnes looked with a haggard eye at Coneybeare, who, mumbling under his breath, didn't seem concerned or angry about anything. He was on his third glass of whiskey, and it was clear to Barnes that Coneybeare was drunk.

Barnes turned his back to Coneybeare for privacy and, facing the Vargas nude, finally unpeeled himself from his sticky jumpsuit. He wished it were the last time he was getting out of this jumpsuit, but he knew it was just the first. Standing in his underpants and socks he tended to the cut on his temple. It was only a superficial wound, Barnes thought. Nothing to worry about. Then he brainstormed: I can tell her that I lost a pint of blood over her. She'll go out with me then. But just so, he remembered her vampire ways, and thought better of this strategy. I wish, he thought to himself, I wish . . . Barnes didn't know what he wished. But he wished that Marie had never voiced that information about the higher-ups. It made him feel as if she were most undoubtedly beyond his range. Everything I ever grow interested in always seems beyond my range. Barnes wondered if there were a name for the syndrome he suffered, a syndrome in which one longs to live somewhere else, even to be someone—anyone—else. It didn't seem so much to ask for—to satisfy this vague longing, if only occasionally. Yet it seemed the dull ache of longing was always hungry and never, never went away. I want you, Marie. I want you so bad. But you seem farther away from me now than if you were lost on Pluto.

Almost every bone in Barnes's body hurt and what bones didn't hurt were sure to hurt in the morning. Nevertheless, it occurred to him that he had just survived—in fact, outwitted—death. And this fact, for a brief moment, exhilarated him. She kissed me, he thought. And that was only a few moments ago. What's more I had the audacity to kiss back! How wonderful it all is. I'm fine today; I'll be dead tomorrow. So be it.

Coneybeare was slumped in his chair, mumbling something about one of Barnes's predecessors—a youngish man who in a like situation (swinging from a rope in the elevator shaft) had actually fallen to his death.

"You're lucky," Coneybeare continued. The sound of Coneybeare's beautiful voice had a strangely calming effect on Barnes. "I've seen guys like you come and go, but never in my fifteen years of working at this place have I seen someone as lucky as you." Coneybeare kicked his foot up on a chair and continued, "You're one lucky sonofabitch, Barnes, and I'm proud to know you."

"I don't feel so lucky," Barnes said.

"Sure you have a few bumps and bruises, but that's not here nor there."

"Pour me a shot of whiskey," Barnes said.

"With pleasure."

Barnes grabbed a cloth that lay on one of the file cabinets and, wetting it with his tongue, wiped his wing tips clean of blood.

"These things," Barnes said, pointing to his shoes, "will never be the same."

"Yes, now they've been baptized in blood."

"They've been baptized in something." "Here," Coneybeare said. He handed Barnes the glass of whiskey. "You deserve it for your heroic deed." Coneybeare raised his glass in toast and said in stentorian tones, "Now let those shoes be baptized in *this* Holy Spirit!"

Barnes took the glass, nodded ceremoniously, then

thanked Coneybeare for all his help.

"Think nothing of it, kid," Coneybeare said with a certain amount of restrained self-satisfaction.

"I mean, thanks for not letting me die in there today."

"It was nothing."

"I swear it was a close one, though. I felt as if I were leaving my body."

"You didn't, though. I was watching you. You just lay there all curled up in the corner of the elevator. Did you see the white light?"

"What?"

"The white light at the end of the tunnel, did you see it?"

"No."

"Because if you had, that would signify you had truly died."

"But I did feel as if I were floating on a river of peace. I had this feeling of joy."

"And that frantic female," Coneybeare said, after a pause. "Truly hellacious."

"What do you mean by that?" Barnes didn't think she was hellacious. Had he missed something?

"You know, the way she screamed so relentlessly. And I thought the alarm from the elevator was earsplitting."

Barnes tried to change the subject. "I'm starting to get a headache."

Barnes located Marie's card and tapped it on the desk. He contemplated, Is it too early to call?

"What's that?" Coneybeare nodded toward the card.

"Nothing," Barnes said. He removed the card and

placed it in the inside pocket of his suit jacket.

"Is that her card?"

"Yes."

"You want to call her?" Coneybeare asked. His voice was slurred by drink.

"Sure."

"Go ahead, then, and call her if you want. Use the company phone. I don't care. Find out if she wants to sue us—the bitch!"

Barnes eyeballed the black phone on his desk. It was durably built as an Eisenhower tank, and probably just as old. Barnes thought back to what midcentury office life must have been like. He imagined a whole squadron of long-skirted female telephone operators filling aircraft hanger–sized office buildings as they attempted to exchange the city's incoming and outgoing calls, each one of them heaving a heavy phone to her ear. Barnes sensed in an almost deep, mystical way that his moment didn't belong in that past or in any other past for that matter (though he wished he could say, past tense: Yes, I've called her). No, his time, his moment to act and call her was now. Fresh on the heels of trauma, what better time? Now or never. Do or die.

"Go ahead. Call her."

"All right." He pulled her card from his pocket. He scanned it. Recto read: "Marie," verso: "Love you. That's: 568-3968." (If Barnes didn't seize the moment—what then? He wished, as she herself had said, that he were a hero—but he certainly didn't feel like one. And after all, what the hell is a hero in this day and age?) He picked up the receiver and began to dial. He dialed the first four digits of her number, took a long sip of whiskey, and felt the whiskey warm the back of his throat. He swished it in his mouth until it numbed his gums (an old trick). He dialed the remaining three digits and let it ring.

What if she wasn't home, what then? But wasn't he too old to worry about such things? Her end rang once, twice, three times and then, both to Barnes's terror and relief, it picked up.

"Hi, Marie," he said, interrupting the female voice, which was, by the way, curiously intimate. Was that her voice? he wondered. He thought back to her embrace in the elevator—her calming tones, her fingers stroking his forehead as he'd come to consciousness. "Marie," he said again, perturbed by his own breathlessness. He'd interrupted her again. He stopped and realized: it wasn't she. It was her answering machine. Strangely he sensed again her shadowy Presence. He thought back to her comment "I know the higher-ups" and felt his heart constrict. What can I possibly give her? I can't give her anything because I'm not in her orbit. I'm not in her orbit because I wasn't born to be in her orbit. She's from the well-heeled, the connected; perhaps she hails from the North Shore. But I'm from Iowa. I'm my mother's child. I'm a failure.

19

Barnes's mind drifted back to the ranch house in Iowa. It had been a derelict, unkempt home out in the middle of nowhere. His mother, though clean and tidy, had lost the energy to clean their home around the time he entered high school. "What's the sense?" she would say. She lost the energy to do just about everything at just about the same time. It was as if she folded into herself and let everything go to hell. He tried to be a good son, encouraged her to look on the positive, but she would have none of it. "Please," she would say in a weary, exhausted tone, "please, leave me. Go out and live your life, Eliot. Be happy. But let me rest. I'm pooped out. Seriously, I'm not joking about this. I'm totally spent."

The home they lived in was built on an infertile plot of soil that no self-respecting farmer would touch. It was surrounded by lilac bushes, and a small creek burbled not more than a hundred yards away. His mother wasn't a farmer. She merely wanted a home away from town. But why, of all places, did she choose this place? It used to drive Barnes crazy that he was stuck out there in the middle of nowhere. And when he would ask her—plead with her—to move, she would make one vague claim or another about the importance of her job. But she had been a secretary all her life, and an unhappy one at that. She also used to say how important it was that he (Barnes) went to a good school. But the grammar schools and high schools he went to as a boy nearly destroyed him. Nobody seemed capable of understanding him. He was too odd for small-town Iowa. "Why," he used to ask her, "why can't we move from this place, get out of Iowa? Or if not out of Iowa, away from this lonesome house?" But his mother had a certain stubbornness, which, though praiseworthy to a degree, was damning in the extreme. And her stubbornness, for better or worse, damned them. He felt ruined by Iowa, unable to crawl out from the shadow it had cast across his life. He felt the shadow of those years now as it fell between him and her. Iowa is the reason I'm working for the Elevator Commission. Iowa is the reason for this inner void. Iowa and my mother are the reasons why I lack inner drive. If I had only had an early leg up, like her. He thought of Marie. Could she really be as beautiful as he imagined?

"Is it busy?" Coneybeare asked.

Barnes raised his hand as if to silence him. "Sh! I'm listening!"

Barnes put his ear to the phone and listened closely to Marie's message. In those same soothing feminine tones, Marie reiterated almost in a mumble the words: "I love you." The voice went on and said, "I love you, whoever you are. I won't forget you." There was a brief pause, then a beep. Barnes fumbled the phone. His voice cracked. He hung up, embarrassed. Coneybeare watched the proceedings and suppressed a laugh, which didn't go unnoticed by Barnes.

Why did I just do that? Barnes wondered. It was too impetuous. It was foolish. Barnes suddenly felt like a human failure. He was ashamed of himself. He tried to forget Coneybeare, the Vargas print, his jumpsuit, which lay coiled in knots and hurled in the corner. He pushed the phone away and got up. He began to pace. He tried to forget his wounded temple, which was just now starting to throb. His whole life had been a failure. He felt he had lived it to the best of his abilities, and yet there didn't seem ever to be any point to it. Why was he such a fool? Why had he exposed himself like this to Coneybeare?

He contemplated her runic words and tried to collect cheer from them. What the hell did they mean? What could they possibly mean? "I love you? . . . won't forget you?" And the way she said them, the way her voice sounded—mumbling intimate tones. It was as calming as water rushing over smooth stones. As if her words "love you . . . won't forget you" were themselves stones smoothed over by years of use. He remembered back to his childhood when, despite his mother's agnosticism, he attempted to embrace religion. Throughout high school he carried a rosary on his person and he regularly prayed the Rosary three times a day because, as he remembered it, it seemed like a good thing to do. There was something comforting in the ritual. "Hail Mary, full of grace, the Lord is with thee." He prayed all of the prayers: the Apostles'

Creed, the Glory Be, the Our Father, the Hail Mary, and Hail, Holy Queen. They were prayers uttered not to any heavenly persona—for he retained aspects of his mother's agnosticism. They certainly weren't uttered to himself either, but they were uttered like some sort of mantra composed in a nonsense language—prayers that were said again and again for the sole sake, or so it seemed, of keeping his jaws from going slack.

Was she talking to me? he wondered. Was I the one whom she addressed in the elevator or was it someone else? Was it the memory of one of her higher-ups for whom she had originally tailored her language? The thought that her words had been a mere reflex, vacant as birdsong, was too much all of a sudden. He kicked the chair and slumped in it. Coneybeare, smelling of whiskey and tobacco, smiled insinuatingly.

"So you get lucky up there?"

"Listen, it's been a long day," Barnes said, trying to push him back. He sat at his desk, unable to move. He thought back to a parakeet he had once owned as a child. He had called the bird Pretty Patty. He had talked to it every day and he tried to train the bird to say: "I love you." But the bird never learned. It never said anything beyond its own birdsong. It seemed incapable of voice. For the longest time Barnes felt an irrational anger toward the bird. He imagined the reason why his bird didn't say "I love you" was because the bird didn't—love Barnes, that is.

"Come on. Get up," Coneybeare said. "It's time to go."

Barnes breathed deep then sighed. "I'm sorry about the elevator. I swear I didn't mean to break through."

"You broke through all right. Now get up. I'll compensate you for a full day."

"How will you replace it?"

"I don't know. I'll have to take it out of your hide. Otherwise we'll hire Ace Elevators to fix it. This building has a fund for that sort of thing. Your job is to keep the elevators clean. Leave the fixing to someone else."

Barnes tied his wing tips, grabbed his empty briefcase, and said, "Thanks."

"No problem, kid. Now get along."

Barnes walked down the long dark corridor leading to the stairwell that led out of the back of the building. Coneybeare followed after him.

"By the way, you're one lucky bastard," Coneybeare hollered.

"Like hell," Barnes said. He felt anything but lucky. He felt bruised and broken.

He banged open the heavy steel door that led to the alley. A dump truck trailing garbage and diesel exhaust disappeared around the corner. A rat clutching what looked to be a human carpal rattled in its wake.

"We're in a rat's alley," Coneybeare said disgustedly.

"Yes, I can see," Barnes said. "I feel it in my bones."

"Guys like you and me . . . always lurking behind the scenes . . . never called to play a part on the main stage."

"But we saved her."

"Yes, she was crazy the way she screamed."

"But it was worth it," Barnes said.

"You're tired is all."

"Yes, I'm awfully tired."

"You should go, get sleep."

"I intend to."

"By the way, Barnes . . . you're an elevator man now . . . count your blessings. . . ."

"Yes. Yes, I suppose I am."

"You're not going to back out on me, think you're too uppity for such work?"

"No, I don't think so."

"Good. Good. Because now you see there's real action at a job like this."

"Is it like this all the time?"

"It's like this from time to time. Also . . . don't worry about the jumpsuit. . . . We'll have a new one for you in the morning, and it'll fit, I promise you."

20

He arrived at his apartment, exhausted, famished. He secretly wished that she'd somehow be waiting for him at his apartment. He climbed the three flights of stairs, his thighs aching from the climb they had made to the thirtieth floor. He was winded, tired of stair climbing. He had spent his whole life trying to climb out of the pit. When would he reach the surface and see the vista of his life stretching off unencumbered by struggle? He thought of Coneybeare's words: "Guys like you and me . . . always lurking behind the scenes . . . never called to play a part on the main stage." He hoped against hope that Coneybeare's words weren't prophetic. But aren't all words prophetic? Barnes maintained the mild superstition that they were. That's partly why he had always been so parsimonious with his own words—lest they upset some karmic equilibrium. He lived in fear of upsetting such equilibriums.

Barnes stood outside his apartment door, gasping for breath. He dropped a cigarette that was clinging to his lips and crunched it beneath his toe. As he fumbled for the keys, he thought—or rather he could have sworn—he saw her face reflected in the brass door knocker. He also heard, or rather felt, her voice. He felt it as palpably as a third presence. It mumbled the mantra: "If they fire you for this, call me." His heart paused. He cocked his ear, he listened closely, in case he had missed something. He heard it again: "If they fire you for this, call me." Barnes was bewildered. He hadn't expected to encounter her this way. Was she some sort of ghost or something? Should I address her—tell her I need to be put in touch with her higher-ups? He thought of her shadowy Presence. Between her and me falls the shadow. He thought of saying a bead or two: "Hail Mary, full of grace," "For thine is the kingdom." The image of Marie on his door knocker and her voice speaking unnerved him. What could it be but a hallucination induced by the day's events? There was the exhaustion, the bump on the head, and the whiskey, which ultimately hadn't settled right. He looked back at his own reflection in the convex brass knocker. His face was glazed, embalmed and projected at a 180-degree angle.

Barnes fiddled with his key, cursed the door, and suddenly it opened.

"Clem!"

He dropped his briefcase, kicked his wing tips into the corner. He undid the tie around his neck and glanced at his face in the mirror. It looked wrecked by the day's events. His hair was disheveled, and there was the long cut across his temple, which thankfully didn't require stitches. There was also a developing bruise on the neck flesh just above his jugular. It was blue at its center and radiated to a pale yellow at the perimeter. It reminded him, strangely, of her eye. He couldn't get over how unsettling her eyes had been. He'd never looked into human eyes and been moved like he'd been moved by her eyes. But perhaps it had more to do with circumstance than with the actual beauty of her eyes.

His ribs ached. His legs ached. His palms were ripped with blisters. In light of his current position on the Elevator Commission, Barnes felt mildly absurd standing around in a suit. I'm such a pretender, he thought. I should be wearing black steel-toed boots just like Coneybeare. But instead I'm burdened with vain hopes. Where the hell did I get these hopes anyway? And why does my life have to be pestered with them? He mouthed the words "vain hopes" to his reflection in the mirror. "That's all you have my friend, vain hopes and a touch of empty ambition. But you certainly don't have what it takes to fulfill your hopes. You don't have what it takes to cut the mustard in the real world. You'd rather lounge around home all day, sequestered from the world. Insulated. Reading your daily papers, watching TV, and letting the world go on about its business, wouldn't you!" Barnes had no compunction talking to himself in the solitude of his own home.

He looked more closely at himself. Am I even good-looking enough for her? Certainly such things as looks and style must count for something. He examined his black hair, which had a slight curl and never seemed to stay in place. He examined the slope of his jawline, which, in profile, seemed to match the slope of his shoulders. And then there was the whole case of his lips—they were thick and unshapely. Where had they come from? he wondered. His mother had had fine, narrow lips that seemed friendly enough when he was a kid growing up. But in her waning years they had collapsed into a tight-lipped frown. Perhaps his lips had come from his father, or from one of his grandparents. Barnes had never met any of his grandparents. He hadn't even seen pictures. Now with his mother dead—and his apparently dead father's ashes distributed with her in her coffin—all ties to the past were gone. Barnes was the only remaining evidence that all the preceding family generations before him had even existed.

He decided to call Marie. Without a moment's hesitation, he walked over to the phone, picked it up, and dialed her number from memory. He held the phone to his ear and listened for it to pulse to life. A woman's voice answered.

"Hello," it said.

Barnes waited this time to see if it was she or her machine. He heard a mechanical click and then "I love you, whoever you are. I won't forget you." There was a brief pause, and then a beep.

Same old mantra, Barnes thought. He couldn't decide whether to leave a message.

"Thank you," he said, his voice cracking on the downbeat.

Barnes walked over to Clem, who lay sphinxlike on the windowsill. He stroked the beast between his two black-tipped ears. "Hey, old cat!"

Clem emitted a mild purr, which rattled deep in his throat.

"Do you have anything to say, ol' puss? Or is that all you

can do, mutter?" Clem arched his back and grew silent.

"Well, I have something to tell you. Yes I do. My first day on the job, and I almost died. Yes, I almost died. And it wasn't nearly so bad as I thought."

Clem seemed annoyed. He leaped from the windowsill and trotted away, leaving behind a trail of dust motes, which seemed to dance like a sort of wild disembodied dervish. Barnes watched the dust motes swirl and thought of the great Turkish mystic Rumi. He knew next to nothing about Rumi, though he did know that Rumi wrote a sort of cryptic poetry popular among acolytes. Barnes had never read a word of Rumi, preferring prose to poetry, nonfiction to fiction, and the information found in magazines, self-help manuals, and TV guides to any esoteric data unearthed from human past and deemed literature. Barnes gazed at the dust that now danced before his eyes—was it cosmic dust from a distant meteor or was it the microscopic detritus left behind by him and Clem as they slowly declined toward death? With a little patience, Barnes thought, we'll both be more dust than this.

In the kitchen Barnes poured himself a glass of chilled vodka. He added precisely one drop of water and a green olive, stirred it with the tip of his finger, tested the martini for dryness, and nicknamed it Sahara. If there were rocks but no water, he would have shaken and not stirred. He wandered back into the living room, slumped into the chair, and fished a cigarette butt out of a nearby ashtray.

He suddenly had the urge to talk to his mother, but his

mother was dead. Barnes felt a tinge of regret and looked around his apartment, which had fallen into shadows. I should clean this place, he thought. In case she ever shows up. But not now. I don't have the energy.

Stacks of self-help manuals and magazines and empty pizza boxes and dirty plates and coffee cups, whose evaporated contents were covered with mold, lay scattered about the cramped living room. Across the room was a full-length beveled mirror. It had belonged to his mother. Next to the mirror was a bushel basket that had all sorts of junk piled in it: his childhood baseball mitt, felt-lined winter boots that were two sizes too small for him, a rusted Zebco fishing outfit that he hadn't used since he was a kid when he used to go fishing with the same local farmer who used to take him duck hunting. Whatever became of that old man? Barnes wondered. Probably dead. Here and there a large black cockroach scuttled in the shadows—and I should do something about them! Barnes had long since accommodated himself to the wayward bugs—they were nocturnal after all and did their business while Barnes slept. What's more, he figured they made good playmates for Clem, though Clem in his old age seemed less and less inclined toward play.

Barnes got up and perused the yellow pages. He searched for her image, but couldn't find it. He even flicked on the television and surfed channels looking for someone—some actress or news anchor or bystander in the shadows—who might remind him of her. But she was nowhere to be found. Those brilliant gray eyes, her smile, the gesture of her hand as she said good-bye—all these things seemed entirely unique. Broken from a new mold. Unduplicatable. What's more, Barnes couldn't get her voice—the low sultry tone—out of his head. "If they fire you for this, call me. I know the higher-ups." And that funny message on her machine, which purred with even greater sultriness: "I love you . . . won't forget you." But what the hell did that message mean? Did it mean anything? Did it mean something? Or did I just imagine it like I imagined her likeness glimmering back at me from my own door knocker as if I were Ebenezer Scrooge and she were Jacob Marley! Barnes looked at her card once again. He held it in his hand. He scrutinized it for a watermark—but there wasn't even that. Just her name, her number, and that strange mantra: "love you." He clutched the card. Could it be this simple? he thought. Pick up the phone. Call her. Make a connection. Say that I'd like to meet as soon as possible. And if she should say, "For what purpose?" Then I'll say, "For the purpose of meeting your higher-ups. Because my situation's desperate. I can't do elevators forever."

In the darkening room, Barnes thought of Marie's higher-ups. Who might they be? The folks with their hands on the lever of power? Or were there others higher up than that? If so, could they—through her intercession—help?

Barnes sank back into the chair, and Clem leaped into his lap.

"Good cat, ol' boy. Good cat."

21

She arrived alive, sybaritic, at half past nine, glimmering on the other side of the old beveled mirror. Barnes looked at the mirror and wondered about it. He thought of the aurora borealis. He'd never seen the northern lights, but didn't they, too, glow with spectral intensity? And weren't old mirrors known to glow phosphorescent from time to time? Something in the composition of the glass? He watched the mirror and, despite the day's events, felt deeply amused. This is wonderful, he thought. I have a magic mirror! He watched the phosphorescent light shimmer across the surface of the mirror and upon closer scrutiny noticed that a woman was sitting on a chair, right there in the mirror. Barnes was astonished. The chair she sat in was like a burnished throne—beyond description. She, too, seemed beyond description. She wore pearls, a glitter of jewels, satin in rich profusion. By her side was a small tabletop and on the tabletop a candelabra with seven lit candles that flung their smoke, stirring the pattern on the ceiling. Also on her tabletop were small unstoppered vials of ivory and colored glass. A dolphin carved from sea wood swam in the same sad phosphorescent light that beglimmered her jewels. She raised her hand once and moved it in a graceful arc. Barnes was reminded of ancient Christian icons with *Pax* inkily tattooed on its palm. She slowly undid her gown, and the silk robe fell to her feet. She was naked but for her glimmering jewels and a dark patch of pubic hair shaped like a diadem. Barnes was breathless. She stepped from her throne, out of the full-length mirror. She was spectral, ghostly, her dove-gray eyes luminous. Barnes sensed her shadowy Presence as if it were a palpable nimbus.

She walked across the floorboards without making them squeak. She carefully stepped around the empty pizza boxes and dirty dishes. She pushed Barnes's hand aside and sat in his lap. His drink was empty. She arrived to fill it for him.

"Love you."

"Yes," Barnes said. "Of course."

"I'm so happy you're alive." She smiled and added, "It was I who breathed life back into you. And I suppose it will be I who take your life away, but that will be a different day. Today I'm here because I love you."

Barnes wondered, Was she speaking in rhyme? He gazed at her and was moved by the beauty of her eyes, which seemed iridescent as pearls, by her smile, and by the pellucidness of her bare flesh. How was it, he wondered, that she had ended up here in his room? How could she have possibly known where he lived—and to have gotten entrance? It was more than Barnes was able to comprehend.

"Then you . . . you have feelings for me," Barnes replied. "You're not indifferent. I mean what happened today on the elevator. You felt it, too?"

She bent his head, as a hairdresser might—with two warm palms pressed gently to his skull. "Let me look at your cut."

"I'm so happy you've come," Barnes said. "I was afraid I might never see you again. I've already called you twice."

"This doesn't look too bad. How do you feel?"

"I feel as if there's suddenly hope," Barnes said. He felt a rare passion—was it love?—brimming to the surface. "I mean, I hoped I would see you. Even though it's crazy. Such hope."

"How about another glass of vodka? A martini?"

Barnes stared at her, his mouth agape. For a brief moment he contemplated embracing her.

"A martini?" she said, trying to shake him out of it.

"There's vodka in the icebox. Do you want a drink? I'll fix it." Barnes made a move to get up. His bones, stiff from the day's events, creaked.

"No, stay here. I know just how to do it. I used to mix drinks."

She rose from his lap, found the bottle of vodka, and poured two liberal shots, each spiked with a drop of water and enriched with a green olive.

"Was that before you knew your higher-ups?"

"Was what?"

"Your cocktail days."

"Cheers," she said.

"God bless."

"Or what do they say? *Nostrovia.*"

"Yes, *nostrovia.*"

They clinked glasses and smiled at each other—she with her knowing smile, and he with a grin that was wiser than he knew. She seemed mildly curious about him. Barnes, on the other hand, was elated.

"Why don't you step out of your clothes, please."

"So you want me?" Barnes queried.

"Please. Before my vodka goes warm."

She stood, turning the drink around in her glass, waiting for Barnes to disrobe. Clem leaped quietly to the floor as Barnes got up and instinctively turned his back to her shadowy Presence and began to peel off his clothes. It was the second time in one day he was stepping out of his suit in front of a stranger. This morning it had been Coneybeare and the Vargas girl. Tonight it was she. But did she—was she a stranger? Barnes tried to reckon it in his mind. When does somebody cease to be a stranger and become an acquaintance, an intimate, a lover? *After all it was she who breathed life back into me.* Barnes remembered back to floating on a current of peace. And though it seemed long ago, the memory of it was pure. He'd never felt anything like that current of peace. And it heartened him to know that when he died, he might find himself floating on that river again. She swirled her glass between her fingers. And who was she anyway, this dark Presence? This knower of the higher-ups? He pulled his socks off, his underpants, his tee shirt. His body was sore, but he felt strangely invigorated. There was a wound across his rib cage, as if he'd been lanced by a sword, and there were marks on his palms—probably rope burns. He turned and faced her.

"Well," she said. She surveyed his concave chest—which was, by the way, nearly hairless. She observed his wounds. His flesh was chalk colored with a purplish hue. Here and there were large fresh bruises from his fall. His skin was yellowed around his armpits. She observed his long narrow arms that angled down to even narrower wrists, which in turn reduced to long bony fingers with dirty uncut nails. He was knock-kneed and pigeon-toed. His muscles—what there were of them—seemed like ropy ligaments that had long ago gone lax with disuse. Though he had tousled black hair on his head, it was nearly bright orange near the pubis. He's a two-toned man, she thought. His penis was shaped like a sea horse.

"If my higher-ups knew I was here . . . ," she laughed.

"Your higher-ups?" Barnes said. He wanted to know more.

"I should introduce you."

"But how do you know them?" Barnes asked. He wanted to know how one came to know such things as higher-ups.

"How do I know them?"

"Your card."

"My—"

"Yes, your card." Barnes pulled her card from where it lay near his ashtray. "This. You gave it to me today. Remember. You said, 'Call me.' And I called, and now you're here." He felt on the verge of laughing at the absurdity of the situation.

"Yes," she said. "My card. I was sure you might be in need of my services." She took a step closer to him and touched his hand. "And of course I may be in need of *your* services."

"But I've no higher-ups," he said, slightly confused.

"Come here," she said drawing him toward her, "and tell me what's on your mind."

"I think you're beautiful. Your body. Your eyes. Your jewels. Everything about you is spectral."

"I'm glad you approve. Is there something you want to tell me?" she asked him.

Barnes, speechless, didn't know what to say.

"I would have come to you sooner," she continued. "But there was some confusion with my higher-ups, and when I finally straightened things out—well it was nearly evening."

"What do you mean?" Barnes asked. "I've been stuck in this apartment for years. It's been the same old thing. Day in, day out. I haven't gone anywhere. Just ask Clem. I nearly haven't done anything, either."

"But you have done things, and that's what I want to tell you about."

He shook his head. "If you're talking about the restaurant jobs, I can explain that. I can explain everything."

"I'm not asking you to explain."

He felt the urge to confess. "I got here. I mean this apartment. It's hard to explain, but I think it's because . . . well, I don't have this—You see it in other people. I mean a sort of inner drive. I don't know where people get that drive. But I've been reading flyers on it. . . ."

He looked at her to make sure she wasn't laughing.

She merely nodded her head.

"I'm all dried up," he said. "It's not that I don't want to do things with my life, because I do. It's just that I don't feel anything acutely, in my heart, anything other than a sense of this void and the terminal end."

"That's life."

"Yes, well. Perhaps it is life. This current of hope and expectation comingled with varying degrees of bitter disappointment and sublime exhilaration. In my case more of the former than the latter. But my bitter disappointment has been caused not by thwarted ambition so much as by the sudden absence of it. A felt void, if you will . . ."

"What you're saying—if I follow you correctly—it's like you're admitting you've lost the will to live. . . ."

"Just ask my cat, Clem. He knows." Barnes tipped his glass. He was pleased by the perspicacity of this shadowy Presence. Not only was she sublimely beautiful, but she seemed to understand. "But we were talking about ambition, not life," he continued. "Though why do the two seem so inextricably linked? Why is success linked with life and failure to death? It's a puzzle that perhaps you with intimate knowledge of the higher-ups can answer."

She smiled at him. "It's a sphinx within a sphinx. A mystery within a mystery that is yet a mystery."

Barnes thought for a moment she was referring to Clem.

"I'll take that as a compliment. He's a good cat."

"And time is a desert that corrodes both life and ambition."

Barnes mused over her metaphor and couldn't decide whether it made him feel better or worse about his plight.

She went on: "You know the story about Napoleon's soldiers shooting the nose off the sphinx?"

"Terrible men!" Barnes blurted.

"And yet who was more ambitious than Napoleon?"

"Nero?" Barnes asked.

She laughed.

"So what you're telling me," he went on, "is the question should be easy to answer. How I arrived here. It's all related to ambition. How did I lose it? I suppose I lost it like everyone else who's ever lost it. I woke one morning and it was gone. As if I'd been sailing a ship my whole life, and then one day the wind went out of the sail. How else explain a loss of ambition? It sounds like it should be easy, I suppose. One day I woke up and it just wasn't there. And I can pinpoint that day, exactly. It was a late autumn day that felt like summer in the morning but winter in the evening. But maybe I never had it to begin with. Though really I'd give anything—anything on earth—to meet your higher-ups."

She stirred her drink. Took a sip. "You're funny."

Barnes was touched with confidence. No need to rush this, he thought. She was a marvel, standing there. Her shadowy Presence filled him with joy. He took a sip of his drink, swirled it around his gums, waited for the numbness in his mouth and smiled. A cockroach scampered across the floor. He took a seat in his chair.

"Hell of a day. But who would imagine it!" he said. Barnes still couldn't believe that only yesterday he was unemployed, with nothing on his horizon, but now—this with her in the room. She with her connection to the higher-ups! How quickly things change.

"When I first heard your voice, I mean when I was standing in the elevator shaft looking down and heard you whimpering, I thought you were just some stranger. But you weren't."

"When you broke through the elevator roof," she said. "When I saw you lying there."

"Yes."

"When I saw you stuck in the coils of rope, bleeding from your head, all because I was trapped."

"Yes."

"When I saw you go through such trouble for me, falling through the roof."

"No, really. You've got it all wrong," he said. "No need to say more. It was my job. It wasn't you. I mean, I didn't arrive to save you. I arrived because I had no choice. The pulleys, the rope. It was all Coneybeare's idea. I fell through because they gave way. We had been drinking, Coneybeare more than I. And he failed to attach them properly. But you . . ." Barnes rose from his chair and stepped toward her. She fell back into the shadows.

"You were the one who saved me. I mean you resuscitated me."

"You've a second chance for sure," she said. "The question remains. How are you going to use it?"

Her eyes blazed as she said "second chance"—a blue phosphorescence akin to the light given off by icebergs when they suddenly tilt. Her radiant eyes were touched with sea green, darker cobalts, and the paling arctic sky.

"You've a second chance," she said again. "How will you use it?"

The question was asked so point-blank, and Barnes, staring into those eyes, could swear he saw an albatross, its wingspan stretching across the waves, gliding, gliding toward him. Barnes didn't know how to respond to her words. It was problematic enough that he stood there naked in the cold, uncanny glow cast by her eyes, but to be asked point-blank questions of life—and not just any life but of his own particularly problematic life. Especially before a potential lover. It was more than he could handle.

"Perhaps I'll go with you. I mean with my second chance." He attempted a winning smile. "I don't know. It was hard enough navigating a path through my first life. However, your higher-ups. I'd give anything . . . I mean I'd *do* anything to meet them." Barnes stood there puzzled, then attempted to put into words a puzzlement that had long ago congealed in his heart unresolved. "Tell me," he said, "about them."

"About whom?"

"Your higher-ups."

"You're cute. I'm glad I saved you."

"But tell me about them. How does one come to know the higher-ups? It's a mystery to me. And I don't know if it's a mystery on account of my upbringing. Hell, I was brought up in Iowa. Or if it's on account of my education, which for the most part wasn't great. In fact it was parochial. Not in the religious sense, but in the other sense. I went to public schools. My education was narrow.

Small-minded. But all my life I've been hearing accounts of the higher-ups. I see them striding the corridors of office buildings. Riding the elevators. Briefcases in hand. The low confidential voices. The polite smiles that keep them at a distance from people like me. I know many are called by the higher-ups. Just like the Marines. And few are chosen. But I haven't even been called. I haven't been picked to be part of the group that is picked from. And that's what puzzles me. One part of me wants to be called. I mean I would like at least to be called. But another part of me—I mean there's a secret part in me. Even if I knew what steps would bring me into contact, I don't know if I'd have the desire to take those steps. Something in me doesn't give a damn. Do you see what I'm getting at? Tell me. Are they happy?"

"No more nor less than you."

"I hope they're happier than me," he laughed. "I almost died today and for the first time in years I felt a sense of peace."

"I brought you back."

"Yes, you did. There's something about you, too. Something impalpable. An emotion beyond words. I don't know what it is—your eyes. Your Presence. If I could do anything with my second chance . . ." He walked over and touched her. "Help me get invited to the game."

Barnes was terrified all of a sudden. He felt cold, isolated. He sat down again and grabbed the martini, took a sip, and let the cold vodka circulate around his gums, then swallowed. Clem returned soundlessly to the darkened room, meowed, and leaped onto Barnes's lap. Barnes sank his fingers into Clem's lovely fur and drifted off to sleep. It was there in that most pleasant of all spaces—caught between sleep and wakefulness—when Barnes dreamt for the first time since her death, of his mother.

22

Barnes awoke, throat parched, head throbbing. It was past midnight. Clem was nowhere to be seen, which meant he was probably in the pantry, second shelf up from the floor, sleeping his ancient Abyssinian sleep.

Barnes was naked, his clothes in a pile by the chair. He threw his underwear on and hydrated at the tap in the bathroom, gulping huge mouthfuls of water, which grew increasingly cold as the tap ran. He washed his face and examined his wounds. His head was throbbing. He took four aspirin for the pain. He examined his face closely in the mirror and mumbled under his breath, "Am I even fit to be a member of the human race?" He had a vague memory of his mom that extended beyond his dream like the heat imprint a hand leaves. What had he dreamt about? Something about his mother. Something mildly pleasant. Had she come and visited him? He walked to the chair, sat down, and tried to recollect his thoughts. He lit a cigarette and stared vacantly at the floor. His hands actually hurt. What time was it? Barnes couldn't get the idea of his mother out of his head. He dashed his cigarette out and decided to investigate.

In addition to the mirror and the baseball mitt from his youth, he remembered he had saved a shoebox of his mother's poems. It was on the top shelf of his closet and pushed to the back behind a bunch of other stuff— hats, mittens, scarfs, telephone books—that he stored up there. He pulled a chair over to the closet, pushed aside the scarfs and things, and found the box. He took it down, slumped into his chair, and opened the box. It was funny. He remembered when he cleaned out her house, he had found this box, opened it up, saw it was a bunch of po- ems, and without reading them closed the box and put it in the glove compartment of the moving truck he had rented for the occasion of moving his mom to Heartmann House, the nursing home where she spent her final days. When he returned to his apartment, he had put the box of poems on his shelf and forgotten about them. Perhaps it was lack of curiosity that had kept him from reading the poems. Or perhaps he just had had better things to do. But now, as he sat in his chair half pushed into the closet, he thought it fascinating to suddenly be examining the contents of this box.

Other than the memory of his mother that he and a few other folks who'd known and survived her retained, this box of poetry was the only thing left of his mom. Upon the stationery was preserved her handwriting, her words, her thoughts. He closed his eyes and tried to remember what his mother looked like, and strangely, no image came to mind. *Mother, who are you? And why this obsessiveness, all of a sudden, to discover you?* He opened the box and brought the letters to his nose, hoping to catch some last vagrant scent of her, but all he smelled was musty paper and a trace of cigarette smoke from his own habit, which he was always vowing to break even as he lit another cigarette. She had her urn full of ashes, he thought. I have this, her box of poems. And I shall direct that when the time comes they be sent to the grave with me so that I, too, have company as I molder to dust. Dust to dust, ashes to ashes . . .

He selected a poem from the box and began reading it. It was a poem about her garden entitled "Pansies." It was a sweet poem with a nice rhyme, that's all he could say of it. He tried to remember if she had ever had pansies in her garden—that's important, isn't it? he thought. It's important that there were actual pansies in her garden, that this wasn't just a make-believe poem about pansies. In truth, he didn't think there had been pansies in her garden. If there had been he would remember. That's one thing he could say for sure. If there had been pansies in her garden, he of all people would know that.

As a boy Barnes made it a point to be able to identify the names of all the flowers and trees. He used to ask his mom all the time what sort of foliage they were looking at. They would walk the property, and he would stop and ask her the name of this or that plant and she would say, "Oh, that's a weed," or "I don't know the name of that one." She knew some of the basic trees: maples, oaks, honey locusts, willows, and of course the lilacs. But he wanted to know the names of all the plants on the property. Perhaps it was because he himself was so friendless—or if not friendless, without a comrade—that he wanted to know the names of all the plants. He remembered a conversation he had with her. At one point she stopped him and asked, "Why are you so interested in the names of the flowers and trees? Can't you just enjoy their natural beauty like everyone else without having to know the names of them?"

And he remembered distinctly replying, "Because I want to know them as friends."

To which she responded, "I don't understand you. I really don't understand you."

To his mom's credit, fair is fair, she did go out and buy him a long narrow book called *Forest Trees and Wildflowers of the Midwest*. Inscribed at the front of the book was the poem—he remembered it to this day—called simply "Trees." As he sat in the closet illuminated by another exposed lightbulb, he remembered the opening couplet:

> I think that I shall never see
> A poem lovely as a tree.

He tried to remember the rest of the poem, but the only other bit he remembered with any certainty was the last:

> Poems are made by fools like me,
> But only God can make a tree.

He quoted a few other stray lines that he thought might be in the poem, but who knows, they might have as easily been from Hamlet's speech (the only other piece of verse he ever tried to memorize: "when he himself might his quietus make with a bare bodkin"). He tried to visualize the "Tree" poem. If you forget something, visualize it— that was always his solution. He closed his eyes and he tried to see it but all he could see was himself sitting here alone in the closet illuminated by that bare lightbulb. Suddenly—unexpectedly—he felt far from home. He felt cast out upon the exposed heath of the world far from the hearth of home. "Home," he said aloud. "Home. Where has it gone and what have I come to?"

He couldn't believe, all of a sudden, that this—of all places—was where he had ended up, crammed in a closet with a box of poems written by his mom. He said that final couplet again as if he were searching for a life preserver on the open seas—"Poems are made by fools like me, / But only God can make a tree."—and he was touched by it again. It seemed so true and in retrospect it was the reason, he realized, why he committed the poem to memory in the first place. He was twelve, he thought, when he first memorized it—sitting outside one autumn afternoon under a tree. And now he tried to remember if this act of memory occurred before or just after he first learned the story of his father. But if it was autumn, well then of course, he was already dealing with the information his mother had given him earlier in the spring: your father, a builder of the bomb . . .

And now so many years later there was this new information contained in her poetry and his growing awareness that, of course, poems were made by fools. He never appreciated poetry, didn't have an ear for it, but he could still appreciate the truth of that line: a person has to be a fool to write a poem. Whimsy must be allowed; without it a poem would never be made. Would the world be a better place without poems? Who knows. The world could probably care less, but would the people who write poems be better without poetry? He thought no. A poem was a place where whimsy entered the world. He thought of his mom's whimsy in writing poems then storing them in this box. It was a gesture against something—a gesture against the end, perhaps. A finger raised in the air to say this is who I am, before I am rushed into oblivion. He had always had such a grim, unforgiving view of his mom, but now, looking through this box of poems, he saw that she admitted a bit of whimsy into her life. She played a fool, at least long enough to eke out this boxful of poems—maybe her garden, too, was a form of whimsy, a type of poem, and maybe she wanted to commemorate the whimsy of her garden with the whimsy of a poem. It was a lovely picture to have of his mom, all of a sudden. Whereas this box was just a box containing poems, nevertheless what could be more foolish or useless than writing poetry and storing it in a box for no one to see? And yet the box survived her, and now the poems were speaking on her behalf beyond the grave. He felt closer to home, all of a sudden. Still it troubled him that she wrote of the pansies in her garden, when in reality there were never pansies in her garden.

He rummaged through the box of poems. He read them in the order in which they were stored, from the front of the box to the back. All of the poems were written in hand on a lovely lavender stationery. Her initials,

JLB, were embossed in the lower left-hand corner of the stationery, and a coiled vine of ivy entwined itself around her initials. He read a few more of the poems and didn't know what to make of them. There were poems about growing corn. She had never grown corn. She grew potatoes but there weren't any poems about growing potatoes. If she wrote poems about her garden, but the plants she wrote about weren't in her garden, then was she lying in her poetry? Were her poems evidence that she was fundamentally a deceptive person? A liar? Here was a poem about a forsythia blooming blazing yellow in the spring and red cardinals in the branches, but there weren't any forsythias on their property, only lilacs. Here was a poem about purple iris growing on the banks of the creek, but he had never seen purple iris on their property, only hyacinths, and yet no poem on hyacinths. What was going on?

It was in her garden, early spring; the two of them were planting seed potatoes. They had been pushing potatoes into the soil when she told him the story of his dad. She had explained to him that her own father had been a shoe salesman in East Saint Louis before he moved his family to Iowa. It was he, her dad, who taught her how to grow potatoes. He had explained how planting a potato was very similar to putting a woman's foot into a shoe: first you dig a hole and then you gently slip the potato into the hole—like slipping a foot into a shoe—and gently cover it with soil.

And so, that morning he and she were slipping seed

potatoes into the earth when she spoke the words that have haunted him ever since: "My boy, I will tell you this once and only once: your father was complicit in the building of the bomb. . . ." Why didn't she write a poem about this? About planting potatoes while discussing family relations who were complicit in the building of early atomic bombs?

Just then, it hit him like a thunderbolt—or rather like a bomb—the stupidity of this story. It was obviously a fabrication. A falsehood. A lie. Or should he call it whimsy? Was his mom joking with him, and he didn't get the joke? Of *course* his father never trailed behind the *Enola Gay*! Impossible. It had never occurred to Barnes before now— what a crazy concoction this whole atom bomb thing was, which she had put together and foisted on him that afternoon long ago when he was impressionable enough to believe every word she told him. For one thing, the timing wasn't right. That was so obvious. He would have had to have been twenty years older for the story to make any sense. Why hadn't he seen that before? Was it because he wanted a story, a picture of his old man, and this is all he had—all she had given him to go on? A handful of fabricated words. The seed of a myth that would grow to dominate his world. A myth slipped, like that potato, into the soil of his imagination, a myth that would over time loom so large he would nearly perish under its weight. For how could he, a boy from the country, raised by a beleaguered mother with no guidance whatsoever, ever rise to the occasion of his father's heroism? He'd always felt a failure because of this very story. He felt a waste. Useless. He felt as if he had missed some sacred opportunity to define himself in a way that a person of his father's stature would approve. He also felt that his pedigree was such that he could never—and should never, for that matter—settle for the crumbs. To do so was to fail. And here it was, exposed suddenly to him while he sat beneath the bulb in his closet: the whole concoction was a myth. A lie. Best-case scenario: it was a joke told to him in a moment of weakness by a grief-crazed mom. But whatever it was, one thing was certain: it was unreal. It had never happened. His father was a whimsical fabrication, made by his mom, like those poems. He laughed now because if he didn't laugh, he was afraid he would cry. No, he wouldn't cry over this. This was a story meant to please. A joke with a belated punch line that took nearly twenty years and a life of grief to reach him.

23

Barnes went to the kitchen and poured himself another glass of vodka, then returned to the closet with the box of poems. He felt rational all of a sudden. A great fog cleared from his head. It was time for truth telling, and he was ready to tell it. If not now, when? If not here, where?

Okay, this is the thing. Secretly, in his heart of hearts, Barnes had never believed the story his mom had told him—or rather, it could be said that in dark moments, he had his doubts. These doubts complicated the whole issue of what to do with the ashes. He had never been certain one way or another and so, periodically, throughout his life, he felt obliged to do something with the information his mom had told him that day long ago: to verify it or discredit it. For instance, he sought other witnesses. Was there anyone out there he could talk to who knew and who could be called on to attest to the facts of his father's life? He searched the town, asking elders, shopkeepers, religious leaders, local politicians. They were all polite to him and unusually sympathetic, but to a person all admitted that they hadn't seen hide nor hair of his progenitor. They were also kind enough, after his inquiries, not to pass around this little bit of gossip: that Eliot Barnes had no idea who sired him. One or two of the people he talked to had an idea who his father might be, but not one of these was willing to face the son and tell him point-blank what they speculated, if not knew, to be the case.

After that bit of investigation failed, he kept quiet for a while and then one weekend, on a whim, he drove to Ames, Iowa, to snoop for answers. He searched the dusty stacks of the library—an elaborate catacomb of neglected books—and remembered only seeing and thumbing through the letters and speeches of Albert Einstein, who inveighed to the great leaders of the day against the doom his theories inadvertently heralded. But there was no record of his dad—or someone like him: a professor involved with the building of the A-bomb—that anyone on campus knew of. When he mentioned the Manhattan Project to the chair of the physics department—a tough, practical-looking fellow—he received a blank stare. It was an agricultural school, after all, or as one administrator patiently pointed out to him: "We study cows and agricultural engineering out here. Or Grant Wood, if one or two of our brighter students gets an idea. But not one of ours was involved in that bomb business."

The experience soured—no, pained—him. Whenever he drew dead leads, he felt wounded afresh—his body cavity ripped open and the exposed nerves dangling out raw for all to see. But on he pressed. He couldn't hide under his shell forever—this shell that was the secret of his dad.

There was that most peculiar time he remembered now, sitting in the closet, his eyes closed, his head nodding after a fleeting memory, when he had come near, if not to his father per se, then remarkably close to Hiroshima. The pain of that memory struck him now, and he felt afresh a sense of sorrow and guilt that he barely knew how to account for.

It happened in between his second and third year attending that major institution. Barnes had taken a Greyhound bus from Chicago to Las Vegas to seek out his father there. As a rule Barnes hated traveling, and his pecuniary situation, such as it was during his college years, allowed him only a cross-country trip to Las Vegas by bus.

It was a miserable ride, the bus crowded, overheated. An elderly woman, possibly in her seventies, wheezed and hacked for breath as if she were dying of emphysema. Barnes turned his face away from her and stared out the window. The billboards along Interstate 80 disgusted him. The factory farms of the Midwest and the barren desert land of the far west bored him to tears. The endless repetition of fast-food joints, gas stations, fast-food joints, and little towns made him sick at heart. It made him wish he had grown up in a different era. He didn't know what to do once he got to Las Vegas, but while he was on the bus, he read John Hersey's *Hiroshima*, to prepare himself, should he ultimately run into his dad.

It was a remarkable book, and he remembered it had made him cry. He was torn by guilt that somehow, by the accident of birth, he was on the wrong side of history. He felt partly to blame for the dropping of that bomb. It was irrational—this grief—but somehow he couldn't escape it.

The woman next to him kept poking her nose over at him and at one point covered her mouth with a handkerchief and asked, "What are you reading *that* for?" In reply, he asked if she knew it, and she said, "Of course. I was a high school librarian for thirty years. Of course I know it."

It was 3:00 a.m. when his bus arrived in Las Vegas. He got a motel room two miles away from the Strip for seventeen dollars a night. The walls of the room were paper-thin with a couple next door—or a threesome or a foursome or was it a brothel?—but the fucking went on all night long without letup. The screaming, the banging, the moaning, the sighing. It made him feel lonely as hell. During the day he roamed the streets, looking for his dad—*Hiroshima* tucked in his pocket. He didn't have any pictures to go on, but he imagined an older man with a younger woman. Was this another myth of his father perpetrated by his mom—the story of the guy who left the family to start a new life with a younger woman in Las Vegas?

As it turned out, there were literally hundreds of these age-asymmetrical couples walking the streets of Vegas. Since Barnes was there specifically to find his father, he was determined to examine each couple that fit this description. Was there one old man among them who bore a family resemblance?

What was the family resemblance? There wasn't much to go on here. Barnes spent considerable time examining himself in the mirror with a picture of his mom in hand—all this while the fucking went on next door. It seemed sacrilegious to observe his mom's image in such a profane space, but this was a circumstance that called for extreme measures. By looking at his mother's picture then observing his face objectively in the mirror, he tried to separate out traits that belonged to her and deduce which traits must therefore belong to his dad. The rings around his eyes, for instance, were his mom's. Too bad, because they were a great identifier—old acquaintances from college who hadn't seen Barnes in years picked him out of crowded streets or bars immediately based on the ring sockets his eyes were stuck in. The cleft chin: well, that must be his dad's. The cowlick and curly hair belonged to his mom, the fleshy lips to his dad. Either that or his mom's scowl had long ago reversed the positive effect of the gamine smile into the petrified frown she wore like a tragic mask to her last days. He figured his dad was probably tall and skinny (as was Barnes) since his mom's height seemed normal. And so with that and a sense that the bony knuckles, knobby knees, and big feet also belonged to his dad, Barnes went on a search. Besides, he needed to get out of the motel—it was driving him nuts.

The problem of the whole endeavor, he soon discovered, was that the passing couples proceeded by too quickly on the street for him to make any certain judgments. Barnes observed as closely as he could all the passersby without being conspicuous. But the sheer number of couples on the Strip forced him to throw caution to the wind, and before long he observed as carefully as he could without worrying how he might offend. By noon, he'd seen many people who resembled his father, but all of the faces he had seen in Las Vegas blurred together into one repeatable face, like the lemon or double cherries spinning round and round on a slot machine.

Barnes quickly realized as well, that his father might be observed walking without a woman on his arm—so his observations would have to include not just males who were attached, but unattached males as well. What's more he didn't know for certain what his father's age was, though he calculated it must be between approximately sixty and eighty. If he were eighty and in poor health, he might not even be seen in public. It was too large a spread with too much variability and not enough to go on. By the end of his first morning in Vegas, Barnes gave up his search. Do I lack the ambition to see even this simple task through? His plan had been to spend the month of August in search of his dad. But now he saw it was a terrible error. He should have thought it out before leaving. It was just like him not to think this sort of thing through, to go out to Vegas on an impulse. He felt duped by his mother's silly ruse. He planned to leave first thing the next morning. He was disgusted. He sat in his room, while the noise from the other room continued unabated. Vehicles outside his window cruised by slowly on the street. He hung his head out the window for a breath of air. In a moment a freakish wind kicked up, followed by only a few seconds of rain— just enough to spatter the dry soil—then it was over. He lay down on the bed with the window open and tried to sleep. He lay there with his arms out and his legs sprawled, and his thinking became increasingly fragmented. As quick as the rain had come and gone, so, too, did Barnes fall into the cleansing sleep of the dead.

In the morning, packing his bags, a thought came to him. As a last hope, before he left, he could at least search for his dad's name in all of the local telephone books. Why not? He had nothing else to do.

But the question was: What was his dad's name? In truth, Barnes didn't even know. It was pathetic. He felt pathetic. To not know even so much as the name of the man who sired him. No matter, Barnes went to work and searched all of the local telephone books with a surname similar to his own. He looked for variations on Barnes. He tried Barns, Bairns, Bernes, Berns, Burns, Burnes, and Barin. This last patronymic was an empty desolate chance, and yet there was hope because the forename associated with it was female, Nel. He dialed the number for Barin and when an old lady mumbled into the phone apropos of nothing, "I said, come this afternoon," he decided it was worth checking out.

The woman who went by the name Barin lived in the desert thirty miles east of Boulder City. Barnes had rented a car and drove out to visit her. The car rental cost him the same as a two-night stay in the motel, but he didn't know how else to get out there short of walking, which, under the conditions—the desert heat and his poor conditioning—was out of the question. Barnes parked the car at the edge of the gravel road and, leaving his bag on the seat, he got out to investigate. Her derelict house was on a wispy parcel of desert landscape surrounded by a fence that consisted of four posts marking the corners of her property and a line of rusted barbed wire haphazardly strung between them. Barnes admitted himself into the yard by pushing a piece of barbed wire to the ground and stepping over it. He knocked on her door with three raps and waited for an answer. He heard something fall inside the house, a vase or something, and then the door opened. An ancient lady in a wheelchair—high cheekboned, weak-eyed—looked up at him from the darkness of her home.

"Yes?" she said through a toothless mouth, her lips pursed into a wrinkled *o*.

It was so obviously the wrong house that Barnes immediately felt like a fool for pursuing such a lead. He said, "I'm sorry to bother you, ma'am," and proceeded to walk back to the car.

"Why don't you come in at least, honey, and visit awhile? I get so few visitors anymore." He turned, looked her over, and thought, Why not?

Inside the house the walls were packed floor to ceiling with family photographs. She directed him to sit down at a Formica table in her tiny kitchen. Without asking if he drank tea, she boiled some water on the stove. She pulled out two plates and set a service of china saucers and plates for cookies. Her movements were simple, unhurried, though her hands were ancient, broken. Barnes looked around the house, waiting for his eyes to adjust to the dark interior. The house was tiny, claustrophobic—lived in by someone who never left. Barnes was used to this type of house—it was like the one he grew up in—and immediately he felt at home.

The pictures on the walls also warmed his heart. In the house he grew up in, there weren't any family pictures. There was only one picture—a poster, really—of a rose, which itself wasn't faded, but the poster had been faded, dimmed, yellowed and dusty, giving the brilliant red rose the imperishable quality of something kept ageless and timeless behind a dusty two-dimensional glass. But as far as photos, his mom had never deemed it fit to hang photos of family members—and that was because there weren't any to speak of except Barnes and his mom.

"Remember, there's just you and me, honey."

"Well then, how about some pictures of us?"

"Because, dear, we already know what each other looks like. So what would be the point of that?"

The old lady set a tin of cookies on the table and asked if Barnes would open it. There was a sense of place and hominess here that had always been absent from his own home. If she was stuck here, he thought, it wasn't by will—more by force of circumstances. Whereas my mom was stuck in her own home by will—or her lack thereof—stuck by virtue of that illness: Life Fatigue.

"My arthritis is such I can't open tins like this anymore. Lucky for you. If it weren't for my arthritis I would've eaten these cookies long ago."

Barnes opened the tin and placed a couple of cookies on his plate. The water in the pot boiled while he sat there looking around. It was a small house. She had a red couch, which was encased in a clear plastic covering. There was a bookshelf with books very neatly arranged.

He looked around and was impressed by the tidiness of the place. Near the window she had a planter with mostly desert plants. He looked more closely at the pictures and saw that the people pictured there were of Asian descent.

She poured his tea and sat it down across from him.

"Oh those," she said, in her voice with that mouth shaped like an *o*. "I brought those with me from Japan. My father, an agriculturalist, moved us from Japan in the late twenties to South Mountain outside of Phoenix. I didn't adjust right away to the desert so I went back to study in Hiroshima, where my family was from. I studied agriculture like my father and I left Japan again in 1938 to come back and live with my mother, my father, and my sister in America. I brought these pictures with me. I snapped them all myself in a weekend, before I left my homeland. I didn't know whether I was ever going to make it back to Japan, so I wanted a remembrance of my family and friends. I had so many people who I loved and who loved me. Japan at that point was my whole life, but my father's produce company was doing very well—he was selling tomatoes as far away as Los Angeles and all over Arizona—and he asked if I could return to South Mountain to help him. I worked with him expanding his business. We worked so very hard back then. Agriculture work, the way we did it, was backbreaking labor. But we believed in the American Dream. We had every right to believe in the American Dream. We were patriots, after all, and what's more, we were getting amply awarded for our labors. Don't get me wrong. When Pearl Harbor was bombed, we were first and foremost American citizens. But Roosevelt made his declaration that if we were Japs we should be interned. It was horrible, the mix we were in, all of a sudden torn between two countries, and all we were were farmers. But we were also, according to the government back then, dangerous. During the war I and my family, we were interned in a camp only a hundred or so miles from here in Yuma County. We escaped the first couple of years of internment by providing produce to the war effort, but in 1944 we were shipped off our land, packed up in a train, and sent to the camp in Yuma County. It was terrible, crowded conditions. We were being guarded and watched over by Americans, but we ourselves were Americans and as I say, we supported the war effort with our produce company. We spent two years holed up there. Packed in cheek and jowl on broken-down beds in animal stalls. I—it wasn't until 1946, we were released. My father, though he tried hard to keep from getting depressed by practicing farming in the camp, he nevertheless died in internment by his own hand. He cut his own throat with a sickle. My mother survived, and I and my sister survived. We tried to revive the family business after the war, but without my father there was no reviving it. I ended up in Las Vegas as a waitress at a small diner outside of town and I worked waiting tables for fifty-eight years. I retired here and remain in Arizona because of my arthritis and memories and because I'm a patriot and no one is going to push me off my land.

"Everyone is different. My sister left the desert in 1947, and she has never returned. She lives in a rent-controlled apartment in Manhattan. Her daughter, my niece, was at the Eastman Conservatory studying organ. Even she won't visit her auntie out here. I don't blame them. I used to go and visit them in New York, but now, well . . . you see. I'm not in much shape for traveling. I'm here alone. But I manage somehow to get by. In those pictures on the wall are my lost ones—my family from my country. My how I loved them. Several of them died the day the bomb was dropped. Some lived six months after the explosion but died anyway. They were all lost. It was so long ago, young man. To you it is a history story. To me it is my life. I can't forget. A bomb big enough to destroy the world— how sad. And I feel, still, heartbroken and sick about it. A suffocating despair I can't escape and which, long ago, I ceased trying to escape. It is my penance for surviving, this despair and brokenness. I hear my relatives talking to me even now as if it were yesterday and tomorrow is the bomb and they will all be gone. Oh! And now I just want to die to forget the sounds of their voices, which are happy voices on the day that I left them. I want to die so their voices may finally be put to rest. And that's all I have to say today, young man. I am not sorry for burdening you with this because it is the truth and it happened and it shouldn't be forgotten. So don't forget. I hope you liked the cookies. Thank you very much for visiting. Now good-bye."

Barnes didn't know what to say or do. He just sat there across from the ancient lady, observing her as she observed him. After he finished his tea, he remembered getting up and picking up what had been broken when he knocked on the door. It was a porcelain vase filled with ashes.

"Here, let me help you clean this up before I go. It's the least I can do."

"Thank you, young man. Just scoop the ashes as best you can and put them in a bowl, please. The rest you can vacuum."

Barnes did as directed, meticulously trying to get every last ash out of the carpet and into the bowl. The rest he vacuumed. What other choice did he have? When he was through, he apologized for barging in on her.

"No apology required, young man. I enjoyed the visit. I get so few visitors."

"I'm sorry then for your hardship. I'm sorry for that. You're a wonderful person, an unforgettable woman. I'm so sorry for what you and your family endured."

To which she responded, "You're such a nice boy. A patriot just like me. I'm sure you have a wonderful future ahead of you. Trust me, I'm a good judge of character. Remember, I served people in that restaurant my whole life."

On the way home, he stopped off in Iowa and spent the day with his mother. The house—like the one of the Japanese woman—was dilapidated. It was a rain-ruined derelict house that should have been scrapped long ago. It seemed smaller and more derelict to Barnes, who was seeing it for the first time since going away to school two years before. The house was all his mom had. She had inherited it from her own father, and she had worked, miserably, at Rural Realty just to keep the household bills paid. Now she was on her own, and the thing had fallen apart sooner than he thought that sort of thing could happen. Standing on the threshold, it broke his heart. He rapped on the door and let himself in. Nothing in the house had changed since he'd left it, it only seemed dustier, smaller. The smell of mouse droppings and mold disgusted Barnes. There was the rose poster in the corridor between the mudroom and the living room. He thought even then that his mom was at the very nadir of her life. How could you go lower than this? he wondered. And yet it wasn't the very bottom, for she persisted in her slow downward track for another ten years before expiring. She had given everything up, just like that. She was suffering from what one doctor later termed Life Fatigue. What the hell was Life Fatigue? Barnes had never heard of such a disease before. He looked it up in medical journals and found nothing on the illness.

She sat on a chair in a dark corner, watching him come through the door. She told him to go back where he came from and leave her alone. He gave her a hug and a kiss, and then opened the windows on the place to let in some fresh air.

"What are you doing?" she asked him.

"Just letting some air into the place."

"I don't want to catch germs. Close the windows. The dust that blows through these things! I don't have the energy to clean. Just close them and leave me alone if you don't like it."

He almost felt like telling her it was his house, too, but it wasn't his house anymore. It had never been his house. He had always felt like a stranger in this house, even as a kid. He thought the furniture was ugly and oppressive. It was all heavy oak with a dark stain. The place was like a mausoleum and just as airless.

He stepped outside into the overgrown lawn and decided to do something about it. He found a scythe in one of the outbuildings and cut a path through the overgrown grass from her house to the gravel driveway. It was physical work that made him happy. He felt he spent too much time in his own brain, not enough time doing things like this, swinging a scythe. He thought of the popular image of death: Death the Culler. Swinging a scythe didn't seem such a terrible thing—a wonderful tool actually and probably ancient, he mused. And then he remembered what that ancient Japanese woman had told him, her own father dead by his own hand, swinging a sickle against his own throat. Barnes winced at the horror.

When he was done cutting his path, he liked the way it looked so much that he cut down all the grass and weeds in the yard surrounding her house. He wondered how long ago it'd been since the grass had even been cut. Probably since he left two years ago. He raked it all up in a pile, found the lawn mower in the barn, put gas and oil in it, and proceeded to cut the lawn to a two-inch height. While he was working and sweating in the yard, a truck pulled up alongside the road. Barnes was going up and down cutting the grass, and an old farmer in the truck watched him work. After a few moments Barnes stopped and looked carefully at the old man. Who was he? Why was he so interested in what Barnes was doing here? He was only trying to bring order to his mother's house. Then Barnes smiled and waved. It was the old man his mom used to meet so long ago on their walks, the guy he shot duck and pheasant with as a boy. He had aged into a sun-scarred old man. His face was as creased as a Depression-era laborer. The farmer lifted his thick finger to his hat brim and slowly pulled away, driving off into the distance where the setting sun glimmered on the heat-hazed horizon like a nuclear explosion.

24

While Barnes was looking through his mother's box of poems, he came across a letter in an envelope. He opened it up and saw it was addressed to his mom weeks after he had been born. It was postmarked Houston, Texas.

Wife,

It is hot here and far from home. I miss you so, I don't know how to put it into words. I was never good at writing stuff. The work pumping oil out of these fields is dirty work and the guy who owns this field is getting filthy rich. I'm only getting filthy. Every day I'm out there clinging to the derricks. Sixteen hours a day. Count them. Six days a week. Rest on the Sabbath. Exhausted to the core. Welp, Eliot's born, God bless him. What can I say? You married an oilman, and I'm proud of it as I hope you are. Tell junior his ol' dad prays that his boy grows to be strong, healthy, happy by the day, and, if the good Lord smiles on him, an oilman just like his poppy . . . or something near 'bouts. It's dirty work but someone's got to do it. I find it's just as good as another thing. I'll be home in June. Be looking for me as you pull the laundry from the wires or as you read this letter, for I am always with you and now with junior.

Love,

Your Ol' Man

PS ~~the oil stains are~~ Guess where the oil stains are from? Because I wrote this at lunchtime.

Barnes examined the note carefully. He read it again and felt a mixture of joy and excitement. What a discovery. He couldn't believe it. His dad's name must have been Eliot, because, as the letter pointed out, he was a junior. His dad wasn't a scientist either, just an oilman. A plainspoken one at that. Almost homely in his speech.

Barnes set the letter aside, his hands trembling for further revelation. He looked carefully through the contents of the box and found something else. In a small envelope, on brittle newsprint, he found the following item—precisely cut from its column in the paper:

On Wednesday afternoon, an explosion ripped through a Standard Oil refinery in Texas City, Texas, killing 15 workers and injuring over 100. This was the latest in a series of deadly accidents at the plant and other facilities on the Texas coast of the Gulf of Mexico, near Houston.

The massive fire from the explosion sent plumes of smoke thousands of feet in the air. Residents up to five miles away said their homes were rattled by the blast, while

ash and debris rained down on the nearby area. There has
been no word yet on the exact cause of the accident.

The phrase "killing 15 workers" had been underlined
in pencil. Barnes read the article again and felt a raw grief
take hold of him. So that's what happened to my old man,
he thought. No sooner do I meet him in one letter, than
a newspaper article in the next envelope takes him away
from me. Life, death—so close together. I hadn't known
him. Then I knew him. Then he was dead. It all happened
so quickly.

Barnes wiped a tear from his eye. So Poppy was an
oilworker killed in an explosion not long after I was born.
Human flesh is so fragile and so is the soul. Barnes's
soul felt wounded, bruised: a great maw stuffed with
questions. Why did his mother feel like she couldn't
discuss his father or what became of him? Why had
she been mum, silent, secretive? Why, goddamn it! It
wasn't fair, her depriving him of his own father—of the
truth—and then only a couple of letters stuffed in a box
I almost threw away. She could have done more than tell
me this beyond the grave. Why hadn't she done more?
Was it too painful for her? Well, who gives a damn about
pain. Life is painful. Look what my father put up with.
Did she refuse to talk of him because he was a common
laborer? Unlikely, Barnes thought. Had she not loved
him? Maybe. Probably. She probably hadn't loved him.
She was too bitter for love, perhaps. Why else would she
have remained mum on the history of his father? Or . . .
or . . . could it have been she loved him too much and this

lifelong silence was the profoundest expression of her grief? Perhaps that's what she caught, not Life Fatigue, but just grief over a broken heart—and the bitterness that comes with being cheated too early of something true—like a young husband's love.

Barnes tried to imagine his father. He couldn't help himself. All his life he had tried to see his father as an older man—a scientist, an unapproachable man, a man so obsessed with scientific truth he would make of himself a sacrifice on the altar of it. He would travel in the wake of the *Enola Gay* and perish of an immolating illness: a slow burn from the inside out. But now, here was new information and it revised everything. His dad had been similarly heroic—though a nameless worker—and he had perished like a torched effigy burnt to ash, the merest statistical detailing of his death charted in the local newspaper: "killing 15 workers."

What did his dad look like? Impossible to say. What was the structure of his face, the slope of his nose? Were his eyes sunk in dark hollows as Barnes's were? Was his posture tilted forward as was Barnes's? He probably wore some sort of uniform similar to the one Barnes himself had worn this very day: a jumpsuit of some sort or perhaps overalls and a work shirt with a name patch over his heart. What did he go by? Eliot? Eliot Barnes? Barnes? Or some nickname that captured some essence of the man but was now, like the man, gone.

Barnes tried to imagine what it must be like walking out into the already hot morning—the smell, the fire and the smoke of the Texas oil fields—walking out there in heavy work clothes, with steel-toed boots and steel safety helmet to work sixteen-hour shifts on an oil derrick. He tried to imagine his father's hands: calloused, wounded, missing a finger or two, the flattened tips of the fingers wearing the horny shell of the toughened nails, and the nails themselves permanently stained black and cracked from the oil. His father had probably been physically strong with powerful shoulders and sinewy forearms. If he had worked on oil derricks he probably had had cat reflexes—not afraid of heights or danger, in a word, brave. And like the very best braves, he had probably been stoic with an overlay of humor to get himself through the day (there was evidence of humor in the letter!)—and what long sixteen-hour days! The fact that someone could write home under such conditions and report that he was happy—it seemed impossible to believe. Yet the writing of that letter, with its expression of happiness, was defiant in the face of what would seem crushing labor. Here it was—the very letter—grease-stained and smudged and yet at the perimeter of the oil markings were the delicate tracings of his father's fingertip. Was it a thumbprint? Yes, perhaps a thumbprint. A left thumb. Barnes scrutinized it carefully. The friction ridges showed radial arc and central pocket loop whorls that reminded him of the cross grain—the age rings, delicate yet sturdy—of an ancient oak. It was a beautiful print nearly immaculate in its detail and it had been preserved intact across all these years. Barnes reached out all of a sudden and touched it gently with his own finger, reaching through time and space into the ineffable regions of ancestral memory to make contact, one on one, physical, visceral, with his dad's calloused thumb. Oh, Barnes thought. Oh.

The letter, the oil stains, they were not unlike the poems his mother wrote. Maybe it was a streak of whimsy in the otherwise bleak conditions of their lives that bound them together. Maybe it was something else. Who can say? It had happened so long ago. They're both gone now—the reasons and explanations of their relationship are gone with them and no witnesses to the event are stepping forward to say what it was all about. Had they loved each other? Was it a marriage of convenience? Had they even been married? Who knows? Who cares. It was their affair, not his, and now they're gone. Dust to dust. Ashes to ashes.

He wondered what his dad might have said to him under the current conditions of his new job. Would he have said, "Good luck. Congratulations, you've finally got a job! Hang in there, buddy, it could be worse: you could be working sixteen-hour shifts in the blazing heat only to die suddenly of an explosion you always knew was out there waiting for you." Or would he have said, "Son, you are mine and you aren't. In the end we only belong to ourselves and we must claim nothing but ourselves as we pass through."

Oh hell. What does it all mean? Barnes wondered. He was tired. It had been a long, instructive day. He folded the newspaper article into its envelope, replaced the box on the top shelf, and without further ado he went to bed and slept a dreamless sleep, curled up under a hand-knit afghan his mother had made for him long ago when he was a boy. After all, he had to be up early in the morning for work and, given the physical conditions of the labor, he needed to be as refreshed as possible.

25

Barnes found that Smith's Brass Polish with a clean soft cloth worked best on the brass doors. He polished each set of doors daily. Since the Elevator Commission didn't have a laundry, and since Augustus didn't feel a need to keep a pile of clean rags around, Barnes brought a supply from home. (Initiative, he thought, is what's going to separate me from him.) He grew to love the delicately filigreed corn etchings on the doors and he loved the elegant egg-and-anchor ornamentation that ran along the top of the brass doors. They suggested a bygone era of craftsmanship. And as if he might do honor to those nameless bygone workers, he meticulously cleaned grit that had gummed up the details for years with a fine brush. He polished each door until he saw his own arm, foreshortened to the elbow, reflected back at him with a dull glow.

After the doors were finished he cleaned the parquet floors. Each elevator had a different wood pattern. And again he admired the bygone craftsmanship. He got on his hands and knees and with a stiff brush and some

Murphy's oil cleaned a decade's worth of shoe scuffings. It was hard work made more difficult by the cramped space of each elevator and the poor ventilation, but he endured it gracefully. He'd never done this kind of labor before (manual) and he was learning that he didn't mind it at all. In fact, he liked to admire the fruits of his labor. It's something people can see and appreciate, he thought. He didn't mind aligning himself with all the other nameless workers of the world who kept things neat and shiny clean. There was a certain camaraderie with the vanished tribe of workers that these elevators represented. He imagined freshly arrived immigrants with sprawling families bringing their inheritance of custom and craftsmanship to bear on such New World contrivances as skyscrapers and the elevators that made such buildings possible.

Coneybeare, who spent most of his day reclining in his office chair gazing in oblique wonder at the posters of recumbent polar bears, occasionally stirred from his position to eyeball Barnes's progress and to deliver one of his patented stem-winders.

"And when you get done with this elevator . . . Jesus, I haven't seen my own reflection in these elevator doors . . . since I don't know when. . . . All the others I would order, beg, and plead. . . . 'Clean the elevator doors,' I would tell them. . . . Sounds easy as pie to someone of your caliber . . . but to all of them it seemed it was the most difficult thing in the world . . . cleaning these elevators . . . because . . . and I'll tell you this . . . I could never get any of them to clean the elevators, and it shows . . . you have shown it shows."

Barnes smiled, but not for long, because with a smile came a new work order.

"When you get done with this elevator . . . I want you to start working on the ventilation system . . . pronto . . . on the double. . . . We have an inspector coming in from the city . . . and he always nails us for our ventilation . . . never mind that he could give a damn whether the things are in working order . . . he just wants the cabins to smell pretty."

There was a lot of work to be done. Barnes always felt busy, never wanted for work, and was worn out come Friday. But when Monday rolled around he was ready. He showed up ready for work with a clean custom-tailored jumpsuit wrapped in plastic. He'd had a dozen made to spec and he kept them cleaned and organized in his own closet at home. He still rode the bus, which was always packed and which occasionally put him in mind of the trip he took to Las Vegas by Greyhound. He wondered whatever became of that woman he had had tea and cookies with so long ago. She, too, was probably dead, her voices silenced, her history lost to his memory and to the few others who cared to think of her. And worst of all, the collection of family photos that defined her existence might now be scattered to the seven winds, while she moldered slowly to dust in the earth below. Or perhaps she'd been cremated. That's what Barnes wanted when the time came, cremation. No fuss, no muss. Certainly he didn't want to occupy any unnecessary space on this already overcrowded globe. And no funeral, please. Definitely no funeral.

The daily upkeep of the elevators provided Barnes with an opportunity to meditate. He wasn't by nature a meditator, though he supposed his daily prayers were a form of meditation. He was too nervous around his own apartment, or too busy reading magazines and pamphlets on self-improvement, to have time to meditate. But this— these eight hours cleaning—this provided him with all the time in the world to let his mind drone on to its own melancholic threnody.

In his cleanings, Barnes often thought of death and of Marie. Who was she? Where had she gone? What became of her? In rational moments he was comforted by the thought that she was probably more normal than he imagined her. She was probably less deus ex machina, more flesh-and-blood human trailing her own penumbra of mortal decay. Other times he felt gratitude. How close he'd been both to death and to her at the same time. And then she brought him back to life for a second chance, and what a chance it'd been! He liked to carry her card in his wallet. It made him feel close, if not to her, to a moment in his life when everything changed. Sometimes he woke saying her name: "Good morning, Marie." He liked to try it on his tongue from time to time. He once called Clem "Marie" by accident. But Clem didn't seem to notice. He lay there as always, his head nestled in his paws, his eyes staring benignly up at his master.

It should be pointed out that one day not long after the Marie event, Clem died. It was a sad day. Barnes had come home from work. It was a Thursday evening, and when he walked through the door he sensed that something was wrong. He looked for Clem in the usual places and found him, curled up, second shelf from the floor in the pantry. He had breathed his last and expired sometime during the day while Barnes was away cleaning elevators. It broke Barnes's heart that his cat had died alone. He had loved Clem no strings attached and Clem had loved him. Clem had been his anchor, kept Barnes coming home every night. Now that he was dead, Barnes felt untethered and worried for a moment what would become of himself. He thought of taking the next day off of work, but he had so far established a perfect attendance record and he didn't want to jinx it. He figured Clem would want him to go to work anyway. Barnes drove Clem to the vet and had the vet cremate him. Barnes asked the vet for the ashes, and he kept them in a small urn, which he kept on the second shelf of his pantry. He labeled the urn so there wouldn't be any confusion should something happen to him. The label said: "These are my cat Clem's ashes. Nothing more nor less. I kept them only because I loved my cat. He saw me through thick and thin, which is more than I can say of most humans."

Barnes wasn't always aware of how completely the ghost of Marie had invaded his mind. He had said the Rosary more than once using her name instead of the Virgin Mary's and he didn't even realize it. Only God knew. That is, if there is indeed a god who listens to such minutiae as guys like Barnes saying the Rosary. Other times, thoughts of her lay so quietly on his mind—like a pleasant melody hummed low on the breath—that if you had asked him exactly what he was thinking while cleaning the elevator doors, he might only have answered, "Her shadowy Presence."

26

Barnes still showed up in the mornings wearing his Universal Blue suit—always ready for the unexpected. He also brought his briefcase, though now it wasn't empty but filled with self-help manuals. He was in the process of writing his own self-help manual. He had no hopes for it, of course—no commercial hopes—nevertheless it was something that gave him pleasure in the off-hours. He liked the form these manuals took. It gave him genuine aesthetic pleasure to read them; what's more, they were instantly nostalgic. Somehow, nothing became dated more quickly than self-help manuals. He loved this aspect of them—this fragile, tenuous grasp they have on our attention only to disappear into the wastes of secondhand bookshops or garbage bins.

It turns out Charles Augustus Coneybeare did indeed have at one time a controlling interest in the Success Publishing imprint. It seemed impossible to believe, but it was true. Barnes had seen his name on the copyright page of several manuals. He was listed as Publisher, Editor, and in several cases as Author. Charles Augustus later confessed that he had gotten lucky with his first published self-help manual. With the proceeds he hired writers to work out the details of several other manuals, so that he could focus on PR and marketing. He ran the business for twenty years before handing over the reins and doing something more important with his life.

"Success was a bootstrapped organization, I tell you . . . and I was damned good at it . . . good at ordering all those writers around, telling them what to do. . . . Hell, there's nothing more useless than a writer, let me tell you . . . ask a writer to come up with an idea that might appeal to the masses, and he's so lost he doesn't know what to do with himself . . . you see the problem with writers is they live too much in their own heads and not enough in the real world . . . I once even mistakenly hired a writer to fill your shoes on the Elevator Commission a few hires back . . . one of the worst hires I ever made. . . . I promptly fired him, but not before giving him the number of a few friends of mine in the publishing racket. . . . Do you know in Hollywood they eat writers up between the salad course and the meat course and spit out the bones? . . . I always wondered why writers had it so difficult out there, but having worked with a slew myself . . . I now know the dirty little secret . . . writers are writers because they don't know what else to do with themselves . . . show me a writer and I'll show you somebody who doesn't know what the hell they want out of life . . . you see . . . and this is why . . . because a person with his head screwed on straight . . . with a person like you or me or the rest of the people out there who are normal and capable of common sense . . . well such a person would never dream of being a writer . . . there's just too damned many other things out there to do in life than sit around and write a bunch of swill that the average American doesn't give boo about. . . . But a person who's screwed up . . . who's been drinking the Kool-Aid . . . such a person thinks glory's to be found in penning his or her own thoughts . . . that the world waits with bated breath for whatever the hell comes to mind. . . . And let me tell you, it's been my fortune in life to set a few of these writers straight. . . . You know what the best part of my job in that publishing world was? . . . It was slapping writers around telling them . . . informing them that the world didn't give diddly-squat about what they had to say . . . the world had better things to do, like go up and down in elevators all day . . . people out there who have real lives . . . real concerns . . . people happy to keep their thoughts to themselves and to a small select few . . . spouses, kids, parents, friends . . . these sorts of people don't give a damn about writers, and why should they? . . . What did a writer ever tell them that they didn't already know? . . . Hell, they're living it, baby . . . they're in the thick of it . . . not just sitting around dreaming of it and writing it down."

Barnes was a bit disappointed that Coneybeare wasn't more enthusiastic about his former business. He didn't even like talking about it. Barnes thought it was an area of common interest, but apparently not so. It was clear from the accoutrements of his new trade (the jumpsuit, the polar bears, the rabbit's foot, the channel locks slung from his belt) that Coneybeare had, ipso facto, moved on from his previous incarnation as purveyor of useless advice that nevertheless hit the mark and made a difference to those in the shadows. Barnes was amazed that this guru of self-help could so suddenly and completely grow silent, taciturn, a whiskey-drinking man of action. It was a brilliant marketing strategy—this going silent—that seemed to impart precious value to the diminishing supply of pamphlets he had already penned. Too bad then, that the supply was controlled by a wayward group of collectors, flea market profiteers, and mom-and-pop secondhand booksellers and not Coneybeare, but as if to ratify that he had indeed moved on, Coneybeare seemed hardly to care who profited from what he had done in his previous life.

It became readily apparent to Barnes that the hardest thing to do was to write a memorable, unforgettable piece of advice. A perfect piece of advice was like a virus that insinuated itself into the reader's memory never to escape. Coneybeare, for a golden period of time, had been replete with such perfect aphorisms of advice. "Admit you're a loser!" was, quite simply, a stroke of brilliance. "Think downward!" was another one. Culled from Coneybeare's own experience, it had a second virtue of being memorable, and though it seemed counterintuitive, yet in practice it hit the mark.

Taking inspiration from the master, Barnes would wait for his own self-help phrases to arrive heaven-sent, and when they arrived he'd pen them into a small leather-bound notebook, a steady supply of which were bequeathed to him by Mia, who was ever curious to see where this new venture might take him.

"Worst-case scenario," she pointed out to Barnes.

"Yes."

"It's a form of therapy."

"I agree."

"Does writing this stuff make you feel better?"

"Absolutely," he told her.

In fact, he was seldom visited by the great storm clouds of depression that had formerly slammed him with such debilitating force.

"You're lucky," she pointed out.

"How so?"

"You have your books to make you feel better. But the rest of us mortals with feet of clay have to rely on medication to make us happy."

The phrases of advice came infrequently to Barnes, often by chance. It was like getting hit by lightning. It never happened twice in the same place and it was always unexpected. "Be ready for the unexpected because it can happen right . . . now!" That was one he would mark down immediately, before he forgot it. Among his favorite pieces of advice was this one:

Are you even fit to be a member of the human race? To answer this one, look closely at your face in private moments and listen to what your reflection says.

It was perfect nonsense, of course, but therein lay its beauty. In the next line of advice he added this:

> But remember—even in our darkest moments, we are still fit to be members of the human race. Now go out there and do something positive with your life!

He found that no amount of tweaking could fix a poorly remembered phrase, so he was always quick to write them down—fresh, unmitigated, as if taking dictation from the gods. In this way, his phrases retained their original perfect form, which for Barnes was the same as saying they were beautiful.

Barnes occasionally tried to share some of his own mnemonic musings with Coneybeare. But whenever he opened his book to share, Coneybeare merely yawned, reached for the bottle, poured a few fingers into a tumbler, and told Barnes to save it for somebody else.

"Can it, Barnes . . . I don't want to encourage you, son . . . because if you were to someday become successful as I became . . . writing advice . . . then I'd lose a great worker . . . and believe you me . . . workers such as yourself . . . folks willing to *dedicate* themselves heart and soul to the well-being of elevators . . . well, let me tell you . . . folks like you are a dying breed. . . . I couldn't stand to lose you . . . and what's more . . . believe me when I say this . . . you're more valuable here than you ever will be as a writer of self-help manuals . . . you ain't no writer, son . . . take it from an old pro . . . one who knows is speaking here."

27

After this comment, Barnes kept his advice to himself and to the doorman in the lobby who wore that red monkey suit with the gold collar tight around the neck. The doorman's name was Alfredo. He was friendly as a warm bowl of soup. An affable guy, he always had a dimpled smile on his face and lived life unplagued by want. Barnes called him Freddy. It turned out Freddy, too, wrote little pieces of advice. He called what he did "fortunes." Occasionally, after work, Barnes and Freddy would meet for drinks at Murphy's and exchange their fortunes. They would edit each other's work, comment on which pieces of advice were ringers and which pieces needed to be discarded. In this way, Barnes and Freddy were able to amass several hundred fortunes and quietly produce a self-published manual—the same pocket-sized dimensions as Barnes's leather-bound notebook, prefaced with a poem by his mother:

> An ear of corn
> Is yet an ear
> Reminding you not merely to hear
> But to listen!

They distributed the manual, called simply *Fortunes from the Shadows*, to the desks of all the higher-ups. In this building alone there were 3,287 souls who composed the set of workers known as the higher-ups. Barnes and Freddy had come in after hours to distribute their manual. Barnes operated the elevator; Freddy had a master key, which let them into everyone's office. Tom and Mia came along to offer support. When they were finished with their tasks near midnight, they went back into the dark bowels of the building, stepped into the oleaginous space of the office, and sat around drinking all of Coneybeare's alcohol. Mia was shocked by the dark musty condition of the space. Tom said it was nothing compared to all the shit holes he had spent most of his life working in. Freddy—who was slightly more drunk than he wanted to be—admitted he collected Vargas pinups, and Barnes countered all of them by pointing out that he was fortunate, fortunate indeed, to be working on the Elevator Commission. He then poured himself two more fingers and went mute.

Within days, Barnes and Freddy could see the results of their handiwork. The denizens of suits and skirts carried their briefcases with one hand and their self-help manuals with the other. They were heading to who knows where, but doubtlessly to the shadows sooner or later. Even Coneybeare was impressed with the results, though he dismissed Barnes as a writer.

"You'll never amount to anything in this field, believe you me ... the reasons are salutary ... you don't understand human nature ... and ... and ... and ... you can't write!"

Barnes developed a habit of arriving fifteen minutes before Charles Augustus Coneybeare arrived so that he could privately change into his jumpsuit. When Coneybeare ambled through the door, sleek as a cat, Barnes went to work on the elevator banks with cloth and cleaner in hand.

The first rush of workers appeared at 7:00 a.m. They were mostly janitorial staff—like himself. Most wore work uniforms of a pale blue or pale green variety. The forest-green jumpsuits were worn only by the Elevator Commission. At 8:00 a.m. the higher-ups began arriving—skirts and suits preparing for another day's work—drinking coffee, plugged into headsets that received either music or telephone conversations, reading the business page of the newspaper, or typing furiously on their handhelds. They got on and off the elevators without so much as noticing Barnes. He may as well have been one with the paneling of the elevator for all the attention they paid him. He had never felt so anonymous in all his life. It occurred to him rather quickly that his strategy of using the elevator job as a stepping-stone was a failed strategy. He laughed at the thought of delivering an elevator speech. It was absurd that he should think something like that might work. But as he cleaned the elevators and kept them in good running order, he slowly began to realize that the world he was occupying was a good world, every bit as interesting and valid as the lives and work of the higher-ups. Twice a week at lunchtime, he would meet Mia. She, too, had a job downtown working at a bank. She was a skirt. The thing is, even though she was a skirt, she complained about her boss and said the work was stultifying. She couldn't stand it. Barnes, on the other hand, didn't mind his job at all. In fact he took tremendous pride in it.

Occasionally he'd find himself looking for Marie. Would he recognize her if he saw her? Would she recognize him? He thought of her words: "I know the higher-ups," then laughed at himself for thinking that she might notice someone of his small caliber. Once in a while he saw a woman who reminded him of her. He thought it was amazing how falling in love with one person could suggest new possibilities of love.

He got on his hands and knees to clean the floors. He cleaned the air filters in the ceiling fans. He justified the work to himself by saying it gave him time to think. He would ride the elevators to the top of the building. Then he'd ride them back down to the bottom. He did this until he got used to each of their personalities. Like everything else, this exercise put him in mind of his childhood. He'd had at least one or two childhood friends who'd been mechanically inclined. He always thought them crazy for not trying to achieve more with their lives, but now he saw the merit in such work. He even hoped to contact them at some point and reestablish their friendship.

Some of the elevators were noisy and banged from side to side in the elevator shaft. Some of the elevators were slow. Occasionally one or two would fail to open at a certain floor, and he'd try to figure out what was wrong with them. Periodically an elevator would get stuck, and he'd have to rappel down the shaft—using the same mountaineering gear he cut his teeth on years ago. He rescued many a damsel, but none like Marie. They were all straightforward cases. Get in. Get out. Move on. He rescued men, too, of course; they screamed, too. The fact is, when the shit hit the fan, people screamed. That's when he went up and saved them. It was all part of the job, no questions asked.

The stairs gave him no problem. Before long, he was in perfect shape and he was agile on the rappelling ropes. He'd been called a hero more times than he could count, and, true to Coneybeare's promise, he'd been called upon to clean executive shit off the floor more times than he cared to recall. The good news was: he had the intestinal fortitude to do it—clean executive shit, that is, off the elevator floors. What's more, he performed this task without complaint. He even smiled at the offending executive and promised that the secret was safe with him. And it was, because Barnes was a man of his word.

Once in a while Barnes visited the elevator he'd broken through. It was marked Out of Service. It was dusty, disused, derelict. This is one I'll fix, he thought. I'm not going to leave this job until I put it back in working order. He felt it important to revive it, bring it back to life. Why not? he thought. Why not? This is where he was brought back to life, and one good turn deserves another. It had a glorious, exceedingly heavy set of vintage art deco bronze doors, which, as he polished, gleamed under the cloth and emitted an otherworldly spectral glow. What's more, it was a one-of-a-kind set of doors, and putting them back in working order just seemed the salubrious thing to do.

The End.

PS: As of this writing you can still find Eliot Barnes cleaning the elevators at 154 S. LaSalle. When he's not cleaning the elevators he's riding up and down the cars in his Universal Blue suit, slipping his self-help pamphlets into the bags and purses of unsuspecting higher-ups.

PPS: Charles Augustus Coneybeare is still there as well—probably drinking his whiskey even as these words are being written.

PPPS: Remember, pull, don't push.

AND FINALLY: Coneybeare had once told Barnes, "Always remember one thing: You're here for the finance, *not* the romance. If you stay here thirty years . . . you stand . . . at your current salary . . . with annual cost-of-living raises . . . estimated at between 2.45 and 3.75 percent . . . to earn nearly a half-million bucks. . . . Do you realize you can do thirty years in jail and not earn a single dime? . . . All told, this seems a reasonable deal, don't you think? . . . And the company you keep is a hell of a lot nicer here than it is in the pen." Of course, to Barnes it was an outrageously reasonable way of thinking about his current condition, and he made a point, on the spot, to mark it down in his book, crediting, as was only proper and correct, the master of the pithy tidbit, Mr. Charles Augustus Coneybeare.